For Made
    FRAN
 in Shenzhen,
1st December 2015.

THE JUNGLE
OF
SURPRISE

THE JUNGLE OF SURPRISE

FRANÇOIS BOUCHER

Translated from the French by
Marie-Hélène Arnauld and Denis Williamson
(Original title: *De ma jungle, affecTUEUSEment*)

Published by Blue Lettuce Publishing ®
Boucher and Luo Infodoc Ltd
Room 9–11, 16/F, Tai Yau building
181 Johnston Road, Wan Chai, Hong Kong

ISBN 978-988-14190-0-2

Printed by Wons Printing Company in China.
Email: sales@wonsprinting.com

Chapter 1

A CURRENT OF COOL autumn air wafted into the hall and caressed her face. A soft transience of September mornings. Léonie abandoned all thoughts of her bucket and cloth, closed her eyes and savoured the moment.

"Morning, Madame Burot!"

"Good morning postman and *be* careful!"

Léonie Burot was caretaker at number 11, rue François Ponsart, 16th arrondissement of Paris and had just washed the four hundred and fifty square feet of white marble in the hallway. The intruder was not going to demolish all her hard work with his ever filthy boots; it seemed that he did his round walking deliberately in the gutter in preference to on the pavement. She went to meet him, with the determination of a brigade of gendarmes halting the advance of rioters.

"OK, OK, I am not coming in. Your post."

"Thank you."

"And what do you think of the new constitution, you're not gonna to be taken in by it, are you?"

"Me? Oh, you know…"

Wary on principle, Léonie was not the kind to divulge her political opinions, especially not in front of a person who could spread them over the whole neighbourhood.

"This referendum, it's a trick from De Gaulle. Fifth Republic? Come on! More of a coup d'état! The People…"

"That's all very well, but I've got work to do…"

Even though the postman belonged to the Communist Party or was it the trade unions, or both, and therefore naturally preached the Revolution (as the Archbishop of Paris preached the love of Christ and the Royal Family the Monarchy) this did not allow him to evangelize.

"All the same, on 28 September you should…"

"Yes, I'll think about it," promised the caretaker and turned on her heel leaving the postman whose affable, but nonetheless affirmed-proselyte's face fell.

The unholy alliance which reigned in this district between capitalism and its victims undeniably posed problems, he seemed to think as he left this reactionary doorstep to go to rue Gustave Nadaud, which probably posed even more.

Not unhappy to have so easily got rid of this nuisance, Léonie returned to her lodge. She threw the letters and papers onto her table, put her glasses on and grumbled. Not sorted, as usual! Would she ever admit that this trivial task of arranging the mail addressed to the dozen or so households of the building was not without bringing her some obscure satisfaction? By doing no more than taking an interest in the stamps and the names of the senders on the back, she guessed much more about these gentlefolk to whom the letters were addressed than they ever suspected. And all this without ever having opened anything, a shameful practice which Antoinette Leroux, her colleague at number 10, was not averse to, on occasion.

"I'm only confirming my intuitions," she would say. "For example, last time, Fortier, the one who always pays his rent late… I was sure that his ex-wife was pestering him with a dodgy story about maintenance. Well, I was right. He's up to his eyes in debt, the poor guy!"

Wasn't she just awful, that Antoinette?

"Ah… but…" The envelope which Léonie had in her hands, of an unusual size, half way between ordinary and half size, bore a blue and red edge and 'air mail'. The stamp, faded mauve and with a facial value of 50 cents, showed the Queen of England in her best profile. It was framed, on the left and on the right, by Chinese characters, and on the top, 'Hong Kong'.

"My goodness! Hong Kong, China! And it's for Mr. Sergent!" Who on earth could be writing from over there to Sergent, first name Jacques, the owner of flat C, on the 3rd floor? Not easy to see: the sender had typed the name and address but forgotten to mention his own. The caretaker weighed the letter in her hand, exposed it to her ceiling light and felt the content, rather thick and protected by internal padding. These examinations gave away nothing about the contents. Hong Kong, though, that was not common. Mr. Sergent, whose annual correspondence could be counted on the fingers of one hand, made up for lack of quantity with quality and distinction. 'Wan Chai Post Office, 30th August 1958,' the postmark showed. So, the envelope had taken almost three weeks to reach Paris. Léonie visualized this long journey: images of liners, planes and maps of the world. Hong Kong... She remembered an illustrated report in *Paris Match*, at Doctor Gilet's, 'A Trip Around The Fragrant Harbour.' Quite something! An amber sea covered with islands, sampans and cargo ships, the streets swarming with people, the strange market places and shops, multi-coloured signs, over-ornate temples, floating villages, the English gentlemen playing cricket on emerald green lawns, and the languorous Chinese ladies smoking long cigarettes, sublimely slim in their straight silk dresses, compared with whom Christian Dior's models looked like tarts...

"That's unfortunate!" she sighed suddenly. Wasn't the man on the 3rd floor, flat C, a victim of what is called the irony of fate, having gone away on a trip the very morning that this rare missive, coming from so far away, arrived? "Well! A little patience my dear," she murmured to the letter putting it away in her sideboard. "You'll soon be with your Jacques!"

"See you the day after tomorrow," he had said to her, very early in the morning, stepping out of the lift with his small canvas suitcase.

"Back to work!" As it happens, her next job is the delivery of the mail. While handing over the Baroness de La Brosse's postcard containing a recipe for ratatouille niçoise, she is already anticipating asking Mr. Sergent: *Could I have the stamp for my little boy?* Of course he would let her have it, she convinced herself while sliding a Minerva catalogue under the Picards' doormat. He didn't look like a stamp collector and would probably enjoy the chance to please children.

Was he expecting his letter or would it be a surprise? This question came to her when she had dealt with Mrs. Couquiaud, the former owner of a big butcher's shop at Les Halles, with whom she always lingered a while. "An eighty-five year old lady on her own," she had said to Antoinette. "Wouldn't you do the same in my place? We chew the fat for five minutes." The play on words delighted her even more because her colleague, with that sluggish bird's face she put on when her neurons were slow to react, had not got it straight away.

Was Sergent's correspondent a man or a woman? Not easy to say from a typed address. But a woman could have perfumed her dispatch. Back at home, she took out the letter and smelt it. No, nothing, perhaps a vague spicy trace. Somewhat perplexed, she went on to dusting her family pictures: her son Frédéric at different ages, she and Ernest, her husband, on their wedding day, twelve years earlier.

"Oops… !" Shopping time already. Later the best bits will have gone, and with the two difficult characters she had to feed… "And if for tonight I prepared sausages? With nice mashed potatoes!" A favourite dish. She grabbed her shopping bag, checked how much she had in her purse, hung her 'Caretaker is out for a few moments' sign on her door, locked it and left. Across the street, Antoinette was sweeping the pavement, in an outfit more like that of a cabaret singer than a caretaker.

"Hey! Léonie! Off shopping? Can you bring me back a litre of milk? I can't get away… a leak in Bastin's flat. The plumber is coming…"

"Idiot!" she thought. The plumber? Léonie dictated *her* conditions and *her* timetable to her plumber. The same with the electrician, the locksmith and all those over-worked professionals who overworked on other people's time. Unless it was not the plumber at all, one had to decode a bit sometimes… Antoinette had a tremendously perverted temperament. What few scruples she had about being unfaithful to her husband did not bother her too much when he was alive, but when he passed away even they had been buried with him, and there were more lovers in and out of her lodge than clients at the DIY section of the Paris Trade Fair. Once, even, she had turned up at number 11 with two guys: Dédé, the latest of her Dons Juan, and another, a stranger with the ridiculous name, Philibert.

"May I present…"

Simply by her tone, Léonie had understood that they were thinking about something involving four people. She

11

had promptly sent them off to take a cold shower. Really, when she thought about it, apart from their being neighbours and sharing a profession, they had nothing in common, she and Antoinette.

There was a queue at the pork butcher's in rue de Passy. Do the Chinese eat sausages? Fish, they do, and even sharks' fins from which they make soup, she recalled – *Paris Match* again – as she passed the outdoor display of 'La Marée'. At the dairy shop, she remembered that they also consumed hundred-year-old eggs. Revolting! On top of the milk for her colleague she bought a small pot of fromage blanc, which she would enjoy with honey, for dessert at lunch. This, for sure, they don't eat!

Back home, it happened without her thinking twice about it. She put down her shopping and rushed to the sideboard.

"Oh, just this once!"

Antoinette, the expert in this field, had said: "With steam it opens by itself, and it doesn't leave any signs…"

Chapter 2

IT WAS A MONDAY. The first Monday of January 1936. During the month that had elapsed since they left Le Havre, Messrs. Bouillon and Vallée had found their sea legs. So, on board the *Hué*, a rattling steamer operating between Haiphong and Fort-Bayard, the capital of the French territory of Guang-Zhou-Wan, they were not seasick at all. And in their cabin which smelt of coal and vibrated with the rumble of the engine, they managed to sleep almost the whole night. In the morning, they would discover a shimmering sea, a golden sun and a glazed blue sky. Then suddenly, almost without warning, the *Hué* ploughed into a grey and sticky pea-souper. Their eyes searched the haze, as the officer on watch shouted through a megaphone, "Land ho!"

"The light house of Naozhou," the voice blared further. The edifice emerged, ghostlike, from the mist. "The island of Egrets to starboard," and "Donghai to port…" Islands? Really? These flat and bare rocks were more like tomb-stones, where skinny cows grazed on meagre vegetation.

Above the *Hué*, sea gulls screamed and would not abandon the boat, as if she brought them their yearly food supply. Vallée, usually so talkative did not say a word, and Bouillon did not try to make him. Both of them realised, with lumps in their throat, that their destination looked very much like what they had read, without wanting to believe it too much, in the newspapers and magazines of the motherland. It was indeed an end of the world with a wretched climate; a piece of land without charm or beauty.

A useless appendix to the Empire too, which, moreover,

was not so gloriously conquered. One fine day in 1898, the *Surprise*, a gunboat of the French Indochina Squadron, arrives. Almost by sheer chance. The boat is sailing in the area and has to take on fresh water. Her captain sends a detachment to land. The local fishermen receive them with stones and insults. Honour, principles… So, rather than go and seek water somewhere else, the captain decides that they must avenge the affront. His men land in force, attack, besiege, and demand apologies before they can leave. Refusal from the local mandarin. The affair becomes inflamed, reaches consular level, becomes a diplomatic incident. A golden opportunity for France. Like the other great powers, she dreams of taking a bite out of China. Since the *Surprise* already occupies this small part of it, Guang-Zhou-Wan, why not appropriate it? So, the land is claimed, reinforcements are sent, two or three skirmishes are won and there is a little looting for good measure. The locals understand this firm language; they capitulate. Paris inherits the place, by lease, for ninety-nine years. A capital is founded: Fort-Bayard. The name is an audacious, linguistic combination of the small fort which the sailors from the gun boat overran and *Bayard*, the cruiser of rear-admiral Gigault de la Bédolliere, who negotiated the annexation.

Shouldn't they have been more wary?

The Chinese standard came down so quickly… Guang-Zhou-Wan? They knew what to expect, they who in the past had deported their worst criminals there and had never managed to dislodge the pirates. Let the French take care of all that since it is their wish to do so! And as well as the deportees and the pirates, other details had been missed. The captain of the *Surprise* had appreciated the deep waters of the bay. The Tricolor Navy demanded to administer the territory so it could serve as a good base for its Far East Fleet. But quickly, it became disenchanted. An almost unassailable current barred direct access to the coast most of the time. One has to tack for hours in dangerous channels formed by the islands criss-crossing each other further off-shore. The *Surprise* had, miraculously, berthed on a day when the current had disappeared.

So the French Navy no longer wants Guang-Zhou-Wan. They pass it on to Indochina. The Governor General of this beautiful and prosperous colony, Paul Doumer, is not overawed: "An inaccessible port, a backward population, mediocre resources... what use could such a hole be to me?" Nonetheless, the motherland enjoins him to turn it into a *centre of economic development!* This future President of the Republic contents himself with establishing a free port, just to compete with the other Chinese ports of call in the area which have expensive customs duties. A few junk owners and a few dubious merchants are attracted. A disparate mob converges on Guang-Zhou-Wan, quietly crossing the Chinese border. France, on this remote boundary of southern China, starts capitalizing on smuggled goods...

It was still doing so. But what did that matter to Emile Bouillon and Gabriel Vallée, ex-railwaymen of the Little Belt Railway around Paris? Wasn't there a fabulous job waiting for them? In Fort-Bayard, they would even have their own train.

Chapter 3

*I*T'S ALMOST TIME *for aperitif,* reminded Antoinette's latest model transistor, tuned to Europe 1: *Better drink Martini, sweet or dry!*

"Am I disturbing you? I'm bringing your milk…"

"Oh yes! Oh thanks."

"And your plumber?"

Antoinette gave a dismissive wave of her hand which confirmed Léonie's idea: The plumber, my foot. Your Dédé, rather! The Don Juan of the hen house had probably decided at the last moment to honour another of his harem.

"Have a seat."

"Thanks. I'm not staying long."

"You have a letter…"

"No… I mean… yes."

The radio interposed opportunely:

Meeting her at friends',
I said to her: Mademoiselle…
What do you do?
She replied, well…

"Ah! Sacha Distel!" Antoinette got all excited. "Such a sexy guy! You do know him, don't you? And listen to this…"

She turned up the sound and bawled at the top of her voice along with the singer:

I sell apples and pears
and scoubidou bee hou–ha!
Scoubidou bee hou–ha!

"Cool, don't you think?"

"Hmm…"

Léonie preferred Luis Mariano and Jean Sablon.

"So, the letter? A mistake by the postman? It's for here? Give us a look."

No, one doesn't say 'give us a look'; Léonie knew it from Frédéric's school teacher. And no, it was not a mistake by the postman.

"It's for Sergent. From Hong Kong, imagine. Because he is not around, I haven't given it to him yet. The stamp's pretty, isn't it?"

"Er… Do you want to open it?"

Antoinette's great quality – and great weakness – was that she didn't beat about the bush. Straight to the point! Léonie blushed.

"No… It's not that…"

"As you wish. But as it happens, I've got some water on the boil for Mistigri's rice"; a stray cat which she fed from time to time.

"It wouldn't be right…"

At number 10, one demolished this type of excuse in record time and without appeal:

"He won't see a thing. And you may be doing him a favour. Imagine if this letter is from some bitch who threatens to turn up from China and dish the dirt on him. He wouldn't dare ask you to intervene. But you… if you know? The first yellow face that shows up, you roll out the canons. Believe me, he will be eternally grateful!"

"Well all right… But promise me that it's the last time you tempt me."

Antoinette suppressed a giggle and prepared to go into action.

"Your envelope is larger than ours. Then there is this padding and it has a wallet flap…"

Grammar may not have been her forte but she had mastered the technical terms relating to her domain of excellence.

"It's not going to be easy," she predicted.

"We don't have to, eh…" Léonie retreated, fearing a failure.

"Oh yes! The tougher they are, the more I succeed! Just watch the artist at work!"

Equipped with simple tweezers, Antoinette juggled with the letter above the steam that she directed by controlling the opening of the lid of the saucepan.

"You see, it must not gush out too quickly." Otherwise the envelope will be damaged.

"Nor too much." In which case one risks touching the inked parts, which makes permanent stains.

"There, you start in the corner…"

It was just a case of letting it open by itself. The back was now two thirds unsealed. However…

"It's not the usual type of glue…"

"Really ?"

"No. Can you pull my hanky out of my right pocket? My nose is itchy. The steam…"

Léonie's hand encountered a muddle of brush, bunch of keys, piece of string, matches, bits of cardboard…

"Hurry up! My eyes too… my fingers… and my throat. They are burning…"

"Whoa… careful, you are going to fall!"

Antoinette fell flat on the kitchen floor. Her body contorted, bright red blisters spreading over her face and hands, her eyes glazed over, her tongue swelled and popped out of her mouth foaming like a giant snail out of its shell. Her friend rushed to her aid, but what could she do?

"Antoinette! Oh God! Answer me!"

A vain request! A last convulsion, a last rattle… Then nothing.

"Mother of God!" Léonie was in shock. Was she dreaming? What had happened, was it even possible? *With the new Simca, the way ahead is safe…* The loud voice brought her back to earth. She stood up, turned off the gas under the still boiling water, and reached for the radio. *With the new Simca, you travel in… krrchch.*

The letter had ended up under the sink, its contents partly exposed from the envelope: a black and white photograph which Léonie pulled out with the help of a spatula. She did not know what to expect but the scene that she discovered seemed to her particularly incongruous; an old steam locomotive was standing in the middle of a forest of gigantic trees. In front of the machine, four people: two men; white. One, slim, in his forties, a thin moustache lining his upper lip, looked impatient; his expression was tense, waiting for the camera to click. The second, of the same age but with a certain plumpness and a complexion one could guess was sanguine, seemed, on the contrary, really thrilled to be photographed as did the first of the two women, a fat European who exhibited an overfed gaiety. An Asian adolescent with the beauty of a precious jewel completed the picture. She purposely closed her mouth as if the photographer had asked her to smile and, modestly, she had refrained. These people were probably there for a picnic, for one could spot at their feet the corner of a cloth, glasses and plates. The whole scene radiated a strange impression; that of a former happiness gone forever, of a nostalgia heavy with hidden menace.

Still with the help of the spatula, Léonie turned over the photograph. Curiously, the back seemed to have been brushed with a kind of oil, on which small particles resembling grains of pollen had burst and formed dark stains. 'Eliane, the Surprise, Fort-Bayard, 13th August 1938,' she read on the top left: words written in dark blue ink, in an elegant yet childish hand, which reminded her of the writing in the accounts books of her seed merchant father.

Was it normal to feel neither pain nor repulsion at the death of Antoinette? Léonie promptly swept aside this thought, for one certainty clearly emerged from the muddle of all her ideas: she had very little time to extricate herself from the mess she was in.

First lock the door. She turned over the sign for visitors: 'The caretaker is out for a few moments' – the same as hers – made by Ernest in his printing shop, and double-locked herself in.

The cause of Antoinette's death? No need to be a medical graduate to guess that: the letter for sure! Booby-trapped, poisoned...

"Oh my God!" Léonie pinched her nose. Wasn't there a strange smell spreading in the room? Quick! The window! She rushed forward only to retreat straight away. If someone saw her? She held back a tear.

"I'm trapped!" Better dishonour than death. So she slightly opened the window, hiding behind the curtain as best she could. The thin stream of fresh air she breathed in calmed her. She cleared her throat, swallowed and didn't detect any abnormal taste. She touched her neck then her chest. No discomfort there, no pain, just a heavy heart.

"Come on woman, there's nothing wrong with you!" she said to cheer herself before lapsing back into self-pity. The police sooner or later were going to get involved. What was she going to tell them? The truth? Unthinkable! Everyone at number 11 would demand her departure. Even Sergent, whose life she and poor Antoinette had, in actual fact, just saved would not be able to defend her. She saw herself sacked, thrown out in the street, jeered at, her head shaved by the locals, just like after Liberation those girls who had slept with the Hun; Marceline, for example, in her home town of Boynes in Loiret province, a friend who had since disappeared but whom people believed had become a prostitute in South America. The absolute shame! Unless... She tried to think up an explanation to an imaginary policeman:

You have to understand, inspector. This letter, how can I say, it intrigued me. Not in the bad sense of the term. To tell you the truth, I found it suspicious.

After all, the fanatics of the Algerian NLF slaughter people and plant bombs all the time. Wasn't it a civil duty, so to speak, of a caretaker to check the postal deliveries to her building? Yes, but no:

Suspicious, in what way, Madame Burot? Are you an expert in these matters?

Or alternatively:

These suspicious deliveries, you entrust them to your friends to open?

Pretend nothing has happened, and quietly disappear? Too risky: she did not remember having passed anyone going into Antoinette's place, but if now, while going out, she bumped into a resident or anyone really: the cleaner, a delivery man, a passer-by...

I'm certain I remember Madame Burot leaving Madame Leroux's lodge, around midday...

Just like the witnesses in *Les Cinq Dernières Minutes*, which she and Antoinette had been watching this summer, in secret, on the brand new Ducretet-Thomson TV of the

22

Berthier's, the owners at number 10, fifth floor, flat C, who were away on holiday in La Baule.

What response do you have to this clear and precise testimony, Madame Burot? The date and time perfectly coincide with those of the victim's death…

Her fictitious investigator alas did not have the perspicacity of TV's Inspector Bourrel. The police surely would not go so far as to accuse her of the murder? But one never knew, miscarriages of justice did happen! Straight to jail! And her husband, and her Frédéric, what would people say about them?

Look, he is the killer's husband! Beware! The murderess's son!

They would be thrown out of printing company and school.

"Oh! It's not possible!" Futile anger. Against herself… and against the anonymous senders of this letter. Who on earth could have planned to murder Mr. Sergent like this, and on top of it all, from China?

Chapter 4

THE *HUÉ* BANGED heavily against the quay, where boatmen in rags, appearing from nowhere, secured her moorings. Her engines stopped. Her gangplank was lowered, screeching unwillingly. Bouillon and Vallée returned the salutation of the two men who, on land, were waving at them. Messrs Claret-Llobet and Pioux, the directors of the Railway Company of Guang-Zhou-Wan and their new bosses, had kept their promise to come and meet them. They had never met before and yet Casimir de Claret-Llobet they would have recognized among thousands: the personification of a castled lord, carrying himself proudly despite his, all things considered, modest size, and what an outfit! Cavalry trousers and boots, ochre jacket, white starched shirt, pistachio green cravat… On any one else, it might have seemed extravagant. But like his physiognomy, it was in perfect accord with his first name and double-barrelled family name and the preposition linking them as efficiently as the coupling hooks between two Pullman coaches of the Paris-Lyon-Mediterranean line. Seeing them, he put on a smile wider than the marshalling yard of La Rapée-Bercy in Paris, more vivid than the rails, baked white hot in the trench of Buttes-Chaumont in July. He embraced them, vigorously gripping their shoulders.

"Emile Bouillon, Gabriel Vallée… ? Our star duo! Our musketeers of the rail! Jean Pioux and I want you to know that we are more than delighted to see you!"

The aforementioned Pioux did not show the enthsiasm that his partner credited him with. He must have been of mixed blood but, with an ovoid torso, stunted limbs and the nasty eyes of an atrabilious reptile, his crossbreeding was not a success. His neglected appearance accentuated even more his overall disharmony.

"Have you had a good journey? Claret-Llobet asked glancing contemptuously at the *Hué*. It's unfortunately one of the few vessels that dare to come all the way to us…"

Disregarding their reply, he invited them to board a carriage pulled by a very dusty horse. An old Chinese man – "This is Pei, my majordomo" – just as dusty, picked up their effects and took the reins. They left the port.

"Let's drop your luggage at the station and go for lunch. At Ping's, the best restaurant in the country!"

And without doubt not cheap, judging by the grimace on the face of Pioux, who must have kept the accounts of the enterprise. Claret-Llobet was above such contingencies; he leaned out of the window and filled his lungs with sea air. Having his fill of iodine and oxygen, he resumed the conversation:

"Where do you come from in France?"

He had obviously not read their letter, in which they had specified that they were both natives of Normandy, Carpiquet for Bouillon, Bagnoles de l'Orne for Vallée. But he was probably too busy. Hardworking Pioux, or someone in the office, must have read through their files.

"You've been friends since childhood, then?"

No. As a matter of fact, they had only known each other as adults, in Paris, at The Little Belt Railway. They had spent ten years together there until the day the line, badly managed and with its back against the wall from competition with buses, announced their dismissal. Looking for a new job, they had leafed through the job offers in the *Bulletin du Rail* and the one from Railway of Fort-Bayard had attracted them.

"We answered it…"

"And I engaged you because my policy is to select only the best. Life doesn't turn out to be so bad sometimes, does it? It's like Normandy. My ancestors on my father's side are from Bordeaux. Bordeaux, Normandy… The Atlantic, the Channel. Almost the same, isn't it?"

They would rather have imagined him, with a name like his, to have been born in some land of plenty.

"I also have a few Russian and Catalan ancestors," he added as if noting their concern.

Their road followed the coast, but the steel grey swell of the sea could only be seen between the warehouses which interrupted the view. Nothing here, far from it, to rival either Le Havre, or Granville, or even… But what was that imposing building, there on the left, which alone compensated for the dullness of the journey?

"Customs and Excise. Very important here… Well, actually, I speak mainly about the adjacent distillery, just behind it. Joking aside, that is serious stuff."

The distillery? They could only see part of a wall. Which alcohol was distilled there? Surely not calvados; they must ask later. Their cart went over a bridge under which brownish water was flowing feebly towards the ocean.

"The Ma-Tse. It doesn't seem much, this river, and yet it's a border. On the right bank they speak Cantonese, on the left bank Lai. People, until not so long ago, still quarrelled over these variances, a bit like the Belgians… But Jean will explain all this to you better than I…"

Pioux frowned. Which bank did he belong to?

They turned off at the corner of a plot of waste ground. 'Rue du 11 Novembre', they could read on a sign riveted onto a solitary pole.

"Patience, it'll soon be built. A future smart area here.

But look we are approaching the centre…"

A cluster of five or six buildings was beginning to appear like a mirage before them. Their guide designated them somewhat wryly as they approached:

"The Hospital, the Bank of Indochina, the Barracks of the Indigenous Guard, the College, and the prettiest of all: the HQ of the Maestro, the Administrator General of Guang-Zhou-Wan."

They were all painted a lime green which contrasted sharply with the prevailing grey.

"Today's fashion. In this climate, no paint lasts more than three years. And, the choice of a colour is a distraction for the civil servants. The thing is, one needs so many meetings and reports to decide whether everything will be blue, yellow or sugar pink! And that's not even mentioning the task of selecting suppliers… So much work for our bureaucrats, and a good opportunity to feather their own nests. Need I say more?"

He didn't need to. Indeed it was the almost total absence of people around that concerned them more.

"Quite normal, most of the indigenous people live in Tche-Kam, about ten kilometres away."

At last they arrived at the railway station, which some sweaty boys were freeing from the painters' scaffolding.

"These half-timbers… they remind me of something," advanced Bouillon cautiously, surprised by the architecture.

"That's the Norman in you! You're thinking of Deauville and you're right. Except that in reality it's not the station of Deauville which inspired me but its exact copy, in Dalat, in Indochina. Dalat! The high plateau of Annam, the Mandarin Road… the mountains, the pine forests, the waterfalls, the fresh and invigorating air! In fact, all the opposite of what we have here, don't you think, Jean?"

Pioux grimaced.

"… It's all very well this chatting but I'm starving and you must be too."

At Chez Ping: salt cellars in the shape of the Eiffel Tower, pepper pots the Arc de Triomphe and white ceramic pots of mustard on checked table cloths; on the walls the Sacré-Cœur, Notre-Dame, the Kina Lillet aperitif, the spring water of Vichy, Joséphine Baker and a wide mural, in the style of a Poussin Bacchanal reinterpreted by a more ribald brush… Apart from the enormous statue of a fat and jovial Buddha who was a little out of place, one might have believed they were at a café in la Bastille.

Claret-Llobet pushed back the horde of waiters rushing towards them (they didn't quite fit into the picture either) and went straight to the back, presumably his usual table.

"Nothing against a pastis, have you?"

"Not for me," balked Pioux.

At just past midday they were the first, but soon the clientele started to pour in. Exclusively men, exclusively French and with helmets which they left on a bamboo sideboard in the corridor. Most of them made a detour to come and greet them.

"Let me shake your hand! Your director has told us so much about you!"

"With this railway, you're going to change our lives!"

They found the remarks of these strangers somewhat excessive, embarrassing even. What could they say in return?

"The prawns are today's?" asked Claret-Llobet, the suspicious gourmet, reading the menu.

The waiter mumbled a "yes" which did not convince him.

"Go and get your boss."

And, the waiter rushed off:

"Ping's real name is N'Guyen. And he isn't Chinese, but Annamite."

As if there were some cheating there.

"… These people are born cooks. That's the reason I'm wary: they could make an animal that's been dead for six months taste delicious. Am I exaggerating, Jean?"

A blinking Pioux seemed irritated. Was he half Annamite rather than half Chinese? Ping arrived, a chubby elf of undefinable age around whose neck a Christian cross was jingling, along with a talisman of some unknown shamanism.

"Today, I'm treating my railwaymen, don't give them gastritis or staphylococci, even nicely cooked ones. We need fresh stuff!"

The owner, servility playing along his lips, assured them that although he was unworthy of catering for guests of their quality, he would do his best not to disappoint them.

"None of your sweet-talk with me. A giant seafood platter and two small bottles of very cold Muscadet."

The order arrived remarkably quickly. Claret-Llobet raised his glass to the train, and announced that its inauguration would be in a week.

"I hope, messieurs, that you are ready."

"For what? To crunch through some crabs or to drive your train?" Vallée said, in a burst of audacity and good humour.

Casimir's response? An interminable laugh, a cavernous gush which resonated in their ears until the liqueur and the cigar with a royal blue band stamped with a phoenix – "A Hatamen from Shanghai, tell me what you think" – which he offered them.

Chapter 5

"HELP!" LÉONIE RUSHED to open Antoinette's door wide. Straight after, grabbing the bottle of milk on the table, she smashed it on the floor. At this very moment, Monsieur Joubert, bewildered, entered the lodge. This doddering old man with the airs of a gentleman-farmer from some operetta and residing at number 10 on the 2nd floor, flat B, came at just the right moment. Léonie had seen him a few seconds earlier through the window, as he was going home. If she flattered him a little, he would not quibble too much about details. Seeing him had made her stop and simultaneously put into place her strategy.

"Monsieur Joubert, you are a godsend! Look what I've just discovered! I was bringing her milk. It's horrible! What should we do?"

"Calm yourself. What the devil are you on about?"

This squire of the salon, who therefore did not make grammatical errors, like Antoinette, ran his fingers through his mane of thick hair and, avoiding the milk which would have dirtied his moccasins, stepped forward just enough to catch a glimpse of the dead woman's feet. The sight was sufficient for him to offer the advice:

"Call the police."

They waited for them together. Joubert, whether he wanted to or no, let his gallantry for not abandoning ladies in distress prevail, when what he really felt like was running away. He was standing as far as possible from the body. Which was just as well for had he gone closer, or worse, shown some interest in the envelope and the photograph, he would have had to be pulled away from

31

them. Although in life he now dedicated himself to no other occupation than that of admiring himself in the mirror, he would probably have objected. Otherwise everything could fit, Léonie convinced herself. She polished her line of reasoning. The letter addressed to Sergent? Any other caretaker could affirm to the frequency of the errors of deliveries. One could not blame the post-office, could one? They all did their best, although one could perhaps, in all objectivity, criticize the rigour of the service. The opening of the letter? Antoinette was an orphan, a widow and without children, there would be no close relative to suffer the dishonour brought by her action, the gravity of which a whole assemblage of circumstances would greatly diminish: quite simply, since the death of her husband, this poor girl had lost it.

There were three policemen, a pale runt of a man and two plump phlegmatic ones; of the ilk of disenchanted council workers. Impossible of course to warn them, *Be careful with the letter.* An immediate give away! But how could she not say anything without exposing them to danger?

"Good morning gentlemen, mind the milk!" This at least might put them on the alert. For the rest, it was all in the hands of God! She would watch their moves and sacrifice her reputation in only the direst of circumstances.

"Inspector Fleurus, from the Criminal Investigation Department." This pompous title under which the skinny man introduced himself clashed with his insignificant physique, yet stirred quite a different memory in the caretaker. But of what, or who?

"Durand and Dubois, my colleagues from the Criminal Records Office," he continued as if this simple statement gave grounds for the silence of the pair, who straight away and without a word went toward Antoinette's dead body.

Name, first name, profession, etc. Fleurus's preliminary questions burst out, machine-gun-like. He wrote down the answers with the help of a cheap ballpoint pen in what very much resembled a school copybook, where his scribbles were packed so tightly that Léonie wondered how he could ever read what he had written. At the same time she was keeping an eye on Dubois and Durand. Or was it Dupont and Dumoulin? Apprehension, panic… such common names and so easily forgotten, they had already slipped from her memory. Dubois (Dumoulin?) was taking some pictures with a big camera with a chunk-phsst which threw phosphorescent flashes throughout the lodge. Durand (Dupont?), attired in rubber gloves and equipped with all sorts of esoteric instruments, was practicing no less singular operations in the immediate proximity of the body. Like a retriever sniffing at the air of the room, he seemed to be suspicious about everything. Still silent, he and the photographer communicated by signs. Yet their robotic approach calmed Léonie. She relaxed her vigilance and came back to Fleurus. Then the memory fell into place. The pointed nose, the pale flesh, the slender silhouette… A Salsify! This is what he reminded her of. Did he also have its brain?

"So you were the one who found the body?"

First serious explanations: the milk she had promised Antoinette who was busy (without mentioning the plumber, real or imagined, unnecessary complication), the door of the lodge ajar, her friend lying on the floor, her scream and the bottle that she dropped, Mr. Joubert passing by, the call to the police…

"The deceased was opening a letter with steam,"

declared Dubois (Dupuis?) as impassive as if he had established that she was podding some peas.

Salsify tut-tutted and moved closer to the gas stove.

"The gas under the saucepan, was it off when you arrived?"

The caretaker, already blushing about Durand's (Dumoulin's?) finding, was on the point of answering no, she had turned it off herself. She stopped in time: the action did not fit her version of the facts. Clearly, there were traps everywhere.

"Yes... perhaps Antoinette switched it off before falling," she suggested, shyly.

Fleurus did not comment. Pilfering from Dupont (Dubois?) the transparent plastic bags where the latter had just placed the physical evidence, he invited his witnesses to look at them.

"Jacques Sergent?" he asked pointing to the envelop, inside which the edges of other photographs could be seen.

The addressee, absent, resided, as one could read, at number 11 and not 10, remarked Léonie who delivered in the same breath the two fundamental facts of her scenario: the post office surely responsible and Antoinette, unfortunately, inquisitive...

"And this photo?"

"A train... in a kind of jungle," she mumbled pretending to discover it only now.

"This grease and these stains on the back, whassat?" Joubert threw in.

The inspector indicated to the lady that the main concern was to concentrate on the persons in the photograph and, to Joubert, that he, too, would love to know. Léonie crossed her heart and swore to never having met, either locally or elsewhere, any of these people. Joubert stroked his chin. The caretaker stared at him, thinking he was about to come out with an enormous asininity.

"I don't know Monsieur Sergent well but couldn't he be one of these men?" rumbled the pensioner.

"Monsieur Sergent? Not at all! It would strike me, I mean…"

Léonie now regretted having chosen such an idiot to partner. With her mouth open like a carp lacking oxygen, she seemed to be imploring Fleurus to save her from the stupidity of the old man. The policeman preferred to smother the growing dispute. He opened up on another front:

"And Fort-Bayard, the Surprise, Eliane, they don't mean anything to you?"

The caretaker was taken aback. Why on earth should these names mean anything to her? It was not to her that the letter was written.

"Eliane, that must be the fat white lump," asserted Joubert. "It's a French name and the other woman on the picture obviously isn't French. As for the Surprise, it sounds good for a locomotive…"

They did not have time to discuss this hypothesis: someone rang the lodge's bell.

"The Forensic Scientist and the Assistant Public Prosecutor," Fleurus announced.

Forensic scientist, Assistant Public Prosecutor? Léonie had not thought about these characters. What was their role? The first, she could guess, more or less. But the Assistant Public Prosecutor? The abstract nature of his title led to complications and annoyances: an inquisitor, a splitter of hairs.

"Doctor Beaumont," grunted the forensic expert, before,

rather athletically, stepping over the puddle of milk to swoop down on the dead woman, as eager as a bear on a pot of honey.

He resembled more the wrestler Duranton than a bigwig from Cochin hospital, although much less cautious: touching, feeling even sniffing the cadaver and its wounds. Léonie was less worried about him – which poison could bother this giant? – than about the two policemen from the Criminal Records Office. The Assistant Public Prosecutor, of more modest build, and sharp features, was called Valiant.

God, let him not be so! she prayed while watching him, circumspect, examine the evidence.

"I must carry out a post-mortem!" Beaumont announced suddenly.

These words froze the caretaker. Their implication both official and anatomic: report and scalpel.

"And these things, they will have to be analysed in the lab," added Valiant.

The lab, didn't that mean the certainty of discovering fingerprints, among which were… hers?

"My brother was in chemistry," informed Joubert although no one had asked him. I know a bit about it myself. With the modern techniques, one can detect almost everything at subatomic levels. And the fingerprints, you are going to love those!"

What business was it of his, the old fool? Léonie could have easily ordered him to clear off.

"The fingerprints, I'm sceptical about," contradicted Beaumont fortunately. If we are dealing with a letter bomb, the person who made it will have been careful not to leave any. Besides, after going through all the sorting and delivery services, in both Hong Kong and Paris, we won't have fingerprints any more, but a purée. And as for chemistry... it's not to be confused with science-fiction."

Joubert did not argue, Léonie was jubilant, the Assistant Public Prosecutor proclaimed his trust in the police and in science, Beaumont announced that he was done when a siren blared outside: the firemen invaded the lodge in their turn. They evacuated the body of the deceased with the same off-handedness as the removal of a piece of furniture, stepping happily in the milk.

And just leave your dirty boot marks everywhere! bemoaned Léonie under her breath. Antoinette's floor would never be the same again.

Chapter 6

THE DAY AFTER their arrival, they paid a visit to the Administrator General of the territory.

"It's his thing. He insists on meeting all new comers. Even I, when I arrived, couldn't opt out. Nothing to write home about but, on the whole, it's quickly done. In any case, don't let it prey on your mind, I'll accompany you."

Claret-Llobet's language had rapidly changed to a slang which surprised them but which they didn't dislike. Vallée replied in a similar tone:

"If he's a nice chap, we'll manage a quick hello!"

"You'll dress up a bit?"

In the end he lent each of them a silk tie, claret for Emile, English stripes for Gabriel, finding theirs "a little obsolete, even here."

At close range, the residence of the Administrator of Guang-Zhou-Wan emitted a kind of artificiality they couldn't fully determine, like a stage set. They went in. An Annamite secretary asked them to wait in an antechamber which resembled a clinic.

"Oh! I must also tell you… the Administrator General, we call him Cod's Liver," whispered Casimir. "When you see his face, you'll understand."

The secretary came back and took them to a vast room with disordered furniture. Sitting at a dark wooden desk, the master of the premises stopped writing and invited them to come closer. The light of his desk lamp accentuated his features and aggravated his bilious complexion. Claret-Llobet was right: the name Cod's Liver fitted him like a glove.

"Emile Bouillon, my driver, and Gabriel Vallée, my mechanic."

It was the other way round actually: Emile the mechanic and Vallée the driver. They didn't mind the mistake. They formed a team. Ten years together on the Little Belt Railway, every day running the same locomotive along the same line; wonderful memories! Going around Paris, doesn't everyone dream of it? La Rapée-Bercy, Bel Air, Charonne, Ménilmontant, avenue de Clichy… Even now, they could have recited, in the right order, the name of each station. Bridges, tunnels, floral avenues or streets of shops, warehouses, factories, mansions… they had digested the scenery over the years until they possessed its essence. And at each stop, with their faces blackened by the coal, there was no shortage of pretty lady passengers to frighten or make an impression on.

Anyway, their respective functions in the service of the railway probably did not enthrall the Administrator General. He adjusted his glasses and, without asking them any questions:

"You are brave… I would like to spare you certain disillusions."

He recalled the conquest and the pacification of the colony, a map of which he pointed to on the wall in front of him. Had they visited the cemetery where the French soldiers killed in the campaign were buried?

"Not yet."

They would go and spend some moments in silence there, they promised.

"Yes. It's very moving."

Cod's Liver moved on quickly, for that was not what he wanted to talk about. For him, what was interesting were the politics, the strategies. The French presence in Guang-

Zhou-Wan helped China maintain itself in the region against the other powers. Unfortunately it played a double game, which is their nature.

"Compromising on the surface but pulling strings behind the scenes. We have even had the honour of a secret society, the Tong Meng Houei, the Society of the Oath! This mishmash of nationalist fanatics and Taoist sorcerers financed by Canton roused subversion by accusing France of practicing slavery. Simply because the administration asks the peasants who can't pay the per capita tax to give three days of work to the territory, big deal!"

Fortunately, the Tong Meng Houei was now more or less suppressed. But other dangers were rising.

"Bolshevik agents, straight from Moscow."

"That's tough," Casimir said sadly as if he were talking of an epidemic of chickenpox.

"What can we do? The local people are so backward, so malleable, so stubborn… they oppose the slightest innovation with an inertia sufficient to discourage those with the strongest will, and complain systematically about any measure taken in their own interest. Their mentality prevents any real progress. We'll soon see how they will welcome the railway. Rather like casting pearls before swine, I'm afraid…"

Emile and Gabriel turned toward Claret-Llobet, who smiled knowingly. With that, their host looked at his watch. Duty called. He got up and guided them towards the exit. And yet he would have loved to tell them about the pirates.

"The other great curse here. It'll have to be for another time."

Chapter 7

Dupont-Dubois cleared off in their turn, and Fleurus allowed Joubert to go home. "How about me?" asked Léonie who was not enthusiastic about the idea of a one to one discussion with the inspector. He wanted, unfortunately, to ask her a few more questions. Among which:

"This Jacques Sergent, without wanting to be nosy, what was his relationship with the victim?"

Without wanting to be nosy? You must be joking! But Fleurus was going to be disappointed: apart from 'good morning' and 'good evening', and not even every day at that, Sergent and Antoinette did not have any relationship. As a matter of fact, 'good morning', 'good evening' was already a lot. It took both humility and spirit from the man at number 11, 3rd floor, flat C, to dare to greet the caretaker of number 10. Conversely, who from number 10 had ever taken the trouble to talk to her except possibly Joubert, the gallant degenerate, whose attention she could have done without anyway? She put on her most obtuse air to convince the policeman of the absurdity of his insinuations. Waste of time:

"I can imagine that your friend was excessively curious. But from that to opening the mail of a complete stranger…"

Whack! She had not seen the blow coming. Yet another detail which, without warning, felt like the sky falling on her head. Antoinette's behaviour, unless she was out of her mind, made no sense if she did not know Sergent from Adam.

"They were not lovers?"

Bringing out the heavy artillery, then? The caretaker almost choked.

"… Madame Leroux could have been jealous, could have believed that a woman was writing to Sergent from Hong Kong."

A woman? Hadn't Antoinette herself imagined the same thing? It was nevertheless necessary to calm the inspector's fantasies. That her late colleague and Jacques Sergent were…

"What you're saying, no, honestly, I don't believe it."

"Why not?"

Because. Full stop… that's all! Léonie was boiling inside for not being able to shout out the simple truth. Instead, prattling which almost hurt her to come out with:

"Antoinette would have told me about it. You see, since the death of her husband, she has confided a lot of things in me…"

Salsify, showing some scepticism, seemed conversely to think that widowhood could contribute to support his supposition.

But he did not push it.

"Is Monsieur Sergent often absent?"

"Let's say once or twice a month."

"In China, sometimes?"

"I never ask him where he goes but to China, I would be surprised…"

One does not go so far for three or four days, the average duration of his travels.

"He wouldn't even have time to get there. Same thing this time: leaving this morning and coming back the day after tomorrow, he told me himself. With a tiny suitcase!"

She fashioned its shape, in the air, with her hands, to give an idea of its size.

"Ok. But letters from China, does he receive them frequently?"

"It's the first time. I mean, apart from bills… The post office doesn't make any money from him."

"You don't think so? What kind of man is he then?"

"Pff…" What to tell the policeman? 'Polite, pleasant, generous with his New Year's tip…' This is how she invariably started describing Sergent when, with Antoinette, they happened to compare the respective merits of 'their people'. 'Sensitive and cultured' she added. Once, he had brought her a postcard of the Opera House, simply because he had caught her in her lodge, moved to tears, listening to a Callas *Ave Maria* on the radio. *For me too, this melody is like a ray of sunshine into my heart*, he had written on the back of the card. More touching than *Best wishes from Le Touquet. P.S. Did you remember to water our plants?*, the usual style of those rare persons who sent her a note during their holidays. This card, she had not shown to Ernest, who would have misunderstood. She kept it at the bottom of her sewing box with a letter from her first love, Joseph, from Combreux, sadly killed during the war. Out of the question for her to unload all this on Fleurus.

"Single, about fifty," she limited herself to.

"And professionally?"

"I think he is in business. But you know, he is very discreet…"

So much so that, for the five or six years he had lived in the building, she did not exactly know how he made a living. "Nothing exciting, a little bit of this and that," he had replied evasively one day when she had carefully sounded him out. He was not like the others, who trumpeted their title of general manager or president of society. Yet, considering the price per square meter in that neighbourhood, he could not be just an underling. All the less possible since he had bought his flat in one payment, information she got from Madame Pinet the personal assistant of Mr. Chevalier, the notary public. He neither worked fixed hours nor in an office, which for Léonie constituted a sign of independence and superiority. He got up early in the morning, went out to buy his *Figaro* newspaper and came back almost straight away, unless he stopped at the café Mozart, where she could see him sometimes, sitting in front of a cup of coffee and a croissant. For the rest of the time, he could spend the entire day at home, or go out again, and come back at three in the afternoon or at midnight.

Wasn't it almost a little comical, thinking about it? Antoinette maintained doggedly that he was a spy. "A queer fish, your Sergent! In my opinion, he's in the secret service." What made her think this? No more than what Léonie had told her about his behaviour and activities.

"His schedule, don't you find it a bit vague?"

There was also the way he had arranged his flat. Or rather had not arranged it. Léonie, whom Sergent requested from time to time to do the cleaning, admitted his Spartan attitude: a table, three or four chairs, a sofa, a bed, a desk… All the best quality, that was not the problem, but cold, impersonal and almost unused furniture, straight out of the factory, bare of any ornaments, photos or souvenirs, as if their owner lived detached, or strove not to leave his imprint on it.

"There you are! He can move out at a moment's notice. With spies it's essential! Don't tell me you've never read that in the papers?" Antoinette exulted, slapping her thighs.

"Tut, if you believe all this nonsense…" And very

quickly, before her colleague had time to come out with another such gem, Léonie moved on to even stranger tales: the degenerate children of the Capillons who offered her, contemptuously, tips worthy of doormen at the Ritz for her to go and get them the latest Mickey Mouse Comic, Grangier the dean, who had a file at the vice squad and a brother hanged for gambling debts, and more: an embarrassment of choices.

"Business… what business? You have no idea?" Fleurus persisted.

Not the shady type anyway, if this was what the policeman really thought. Or… that Sergent may not have been completely kosher intrigued her for a moment. But of course not! What was she thinking? She chastised herself for her disloyalty.

"Fine, I'll ask the man himself directly. Let me know when he shows up again."

Salsify meticulously tore out a quarter of a page of his copybook.

"Sorry, I'm short of name cards…"

Félix Fleurus, Police Inspector, Criminal Investigation Department, he wrote carefully to be legible. Adding a phone number where, he assured her, he could be contacted at any time.

Félix Fleurus. Léonie tried to imagine: if her name were Fleurus, would the idea of calling her son Félix ever have occurred to her? But there again, she had known a Jeanine Jeannot at school. It just shows you…

Chapter 8

"**T**HAT GENTLEMAN is an idiot!"

Emile and Gabriel wondered. Who was their employer criticizing in this way? Cod's Liver?

"Precisely! Cod's Liver, the chief of the territory, or who pretends to be. But still, an idiot…" And even those who called him that were offering him a compliment, as the truth lay far beyond the meaning of this oft-used word. Hadn't they listened the slightest bit to the ramblings of the half-wit they had just left? The spongy substance filling his head formed a desert even more staggering than the Gobi and the Taklamakan joined together. *Classic of the Perfect Emptiness*… Lieh Tzu.

The railway manager paused, as if taking the time to choose the best in a catalogue of innumerable references.

"Here you are, one proof among thousands… The famous pirates he had the pretension to mention to you. He has never seen more than a photograph of them. All the same, he had the audacity, last year, to think up a plan to annihilate them… Quite proud, the fool! He unveiled it at the 14th of July celebrations, between two petits fours. He was guaranteeing the eradication of the rogues within six months. What a promise! Listen to this, gentlemen…"

Claret-Llobet, animated by a fervent merriment, started to shake his left thumb, imprisoned within his right hand, as if it were a party bomb full of assorted streamers. Look out! He was going to let the thing go, it was going to explode, they would have a good laugh…

"First of all, taking a census of all the men aged between eighteen and fifty, for as everyone knows the pirates are hiding among the population…"

He abandoned his thumb for his forefinger. What was to follow promised to be even more devastating.

"Second, marking the livestock and forbidding the trade in women and children, over the whole territory, in order to dry up the main income of the traffickers at its source…"

Emile and Gabriel smiled politely. They did not judge these propositions as being so unreasonable. But Casimir had strength in reserve; the stupidity of Cod's Liver would become obvious to them imminently.

"Third, the beggar wanted to apply Chinese criminal law to the pirates. You hear that? Chinese criminal law! You should have seen Amyot's face, the engineer from Public Works… that's the chap who's also the representative of the League of Human Rights or some such garrulous sect. He was already imagining torture and slow death on the public square in Fort-Bayard. Well, all right, it wasn't quite that which our hothead was cooking up; but he did plan to make the families responsible for their black sheep. Like under the Tang Dynasty: 'There is at least one pirate in each household of Guang-Zhou-Wan. From now on, parents will pay for the criminal acts of their children, and vice-versa.' 'It's unconstitutional!' shouted Amyot. 'It's, above all, very stupid,' I replied. 'It'll turn all the plebs against us!' Fortunately here, one talks a lot but doesn't do much. The prat has never carried out a fraction of his crazy ideas."

QED. The Administrator General was an idiot. An idiot who, on top of this, did not like him. This, they could not but have noticed:

"My train casting pearls before swine? The truth is, he is worried that the railway may cause him to lose some of his power. The little he has… He dreams of Fort-Bayard as being self-sufficient, walled in and without contact with China; so massive, so threatening. In fact, he has already damaged our business in Tche-Kam, the Chinese town, which, I'd like to point out, has twice the population of Fort-Bayard. I wanted the train to stop there. Our Chinese also have the right to go to China, don't they? Cod's Liver thinks the contrary. Tche-Kam, for him? A centre of perpetual rebellion, a den of bandits, the dregs of the colony. I could go on. 'Get the railway running over there? Too dangerous!' This is what this imbecile wrote to the banks and shareholders. All because two or three naive Europeans were robbed there, and because they don't kowtow to the French Republic. The result: those gentlemen of finance have very kindly asked me to modify my route otherwise they wouldn't break open their piggy banks. But you, do you think it's fair to deprive a railway company of half its customers?"

Bouillon and Vallée were discovering these past squabbles with amazement. If Claret-Llobet was telling the truth… They dared not explicitly ask but… Wasn't the profitability of the line in jeopardy?

"Don't worry! We'll still manage!"

And on top of that, regarding Cod's Liver:

"I too have friends in high places. One of these days, I'm going to have him shown the door, this good-for-nothing!"

Chapter 9

THE NEWS OF ANTOINETTE'S death spread around the district as rapidly as the tide around Mont Saint-Michel, causing a long procession of visitors towards Léonie's. All the residents of number 10, number 11 and even of the whole street and beyond who were at home in the afternoon – in other words all those with nothing to do, pensioners and convalescents with time to spare – knocked on her window to be told about the drama. To the first ones, she confided willingly, perhaps to avoid brooding on it herself. Her public commiserated with her:

"What an ordeal, to discover a body! And of a friend as well!"

"And to be interrogated by the police!"

"Were they polite, at least?"

She knew these two-faced people well. Should they spot the slightest contradiction in her story they would metamorphose their comments into unrestrained viperous gossip. She controlled her nerves and was careful not to contradict herself: wouldn't her truth become, progressively, The Truth? Unfortunately, in repeating the same thing ten or twelve times, one ends up getting rather tired of the whole thing. She wished she could close her door to the curious. A decision more difficult than one might think. Those from number 11? Impossible, because of the management system, she was indirectly their employee. Those at number 10? They had just lost their caretaker and merited a minimum of consideration. The others? The less people could legitimately claim a right, a service or a favour, the more aggressive they proved to be when refused it. While talking, she started to reflect on the police enquiry. Well, according to the forensic expert, they would not be able to detect usable fingerprints on the letter. But weren't there other means of unmasking her? The inspector would, without doubt, go to the post office and grill the postman who would of course deny all error of delivery. He would hide behind the logic:

A letter from Hong Kong, indeed I remember! They don't come everyday! I am absolutely sure I gave it to Madame Burot.

How would she defend herself? With her savings she could scarcely afford a lawyer, and especially not Lepeltier, 3rd floor, flat A; among the meanest with his New Year's tips, so he wouldn't offer her a discount. Even if he did, his fees would still be exorbitant… "A dress from Chanel with even a 50% reduction would cost us only one year's salary instead of two," Antoinette often joked. In any case, probably Lepeltier did not stoop so low as to defend caretakers. Life was indeed too unjust, and she was finished. Again the visions of her son humiliated at school, of Ernest sacked, of herself kicked out like a criminal and her hair shaven in front of everyone. Like Marceline. She burst into tears. Her visitors of the moment, the Leognan sisters, two spinsters from the top of rue de la Pompe, left straight away. They had come to be terrified, not to comfort a soul mourning a loss.

Just as well! Léonie shut herself away at home and decided to play dead, if one could say so without offending the memory of Antoinette.

A quarter past four. She splashed her face with water to remove all trace of tears. It was time to go and pick up Frédéric from school, rue des Bauches. She arrived as if nothing had happened… But as soon as the usual hive of mothers and maids buzzing in front of the building saw her, they assailed her. She thought she had found a suitable retort by articulating the obligation of discretion set by the police. The questions however continued more than ever:

"So, it's a murder, is it?"

"Have you any idea who could have done it?"

Frédéric arrived at last, chatting with his best friend Michel Aubry.

"Tomorrow, tell us all about it, eh?" she heard the boy say before they parted. She planted a kiss on her son's forehead, only slightly tender, because he was opposed to demonstrations of affection in public, and they walked away.

"Did you have a good day?"

"Mmm…"

"A lot of homework?"

"So so."

She thought herself foolish. Frédéric knew! The request from his friend could only have something to do with that. They walked past the bakery The Golden Brioche in the alley La Muette. The baker saw them and pointed them out to her clients. Six pairs of eyes focused on them. Léonie strongly grasped Frédéric's hand, pulled him towards her and quickened her pace.

"Mum, is it true someone killed Antoinette, and that it's you who found her body?"

"Where did you get that from?"

"I er… heard the headmaster during playtime. He was talking about it with the teachers and they were all looking at me as if I had fleas…"

Léonie would have loved to see them all pilloried.

"They were saying that Antoinette was poisoned by a letter coming from China."

"Apparently."

"I'm not surprised."

"What do you mean, you're not surprised?"

"No. I saw a Chinese man, not so long ago…"

"What?" What was Frédéric talking about? Léonie wanted to reassure herself: the foreign population was not numerous in the area, but two or three Asians did wander around from time to time. The Chinese of her son must be one of them. Nevertheless…

"Remember, once, I came back early from catechism. You had gone out shopping."

"And?"

"He was in the building…"

"My god! And what was he doing?"

"He was writing down the names of the residents."

Chapter 10

CLARET-LLOBET HAD bought his three carriages second hand, olive green English Leightons, from the Kowloon-Canton Railway Corporation. "Basic but in perfect working order, and quite sufficient to begin with. A bloody good investment!" As for the locomotive, a twenty-five ton Hohenzollern, whose whole career had been in Japan. "On a line in Hokkaido, snowed up all year round. She endured for more than twenty years in this environment. You can imagine that here she'll enjoy it much better!" Not a young lass anymore though, the railwaymen concluded. But their boss could be right: second hand engines sometimes had some nice hidden surprises.

Last minute adjustments, dry runs... They worked relentlessly all week long. On the eve of the inauguration, they affixed a crown of flowers to the nose of the boiler, and French flags to the four corners of the cabin.

On the big day, at zero hour, the whole of Fort-Bayard had converged on the railway. A fascinating procession, undulating like a caterpillar through the overheated streets of the town. Leading the way, a multicoloured dragon danced to a Chinese fanfare: deafening cymbals, shrill recorders and bursts of firecrackers. Following on, in three or four cleverly combined rows, were the helmets, the two-pointed hats, the coats, the uniforms and the decorations of the colonials, the hats with feathers and the embroidered dresses of the mandarins. Casimir flitted from one row to the next, like a drunken butterfly. Behind this assemblage came the spouses and relatives, the elegance of the west jousting with that of the east: frills with silks, Parisian parasols with Pekinese, ruby with jade. This high society entered the great hall of the station which smelt of wet paint and varnished panelling. Officials climbed up to the rostrum decked out in red, white and blue and erected in the middle of the room. Speech! Casimir, brief and humble, thanked his father and mother and all those who had supported him. The president of the Chamber of Commerce launched into a eulogy to France and to China, then onto business and to trains, the latter of which allowed more of the former to be carried out and more quickly. Cod's Liver, to finish with, listed progress, civilization, modern life and other solemnities heard a thousand times before but which made a good impression and which Claret-Llobet encouraged people to applaud noisily before inviting the guests to move to the platform and embark. It took half an hour of manoeuvre and negotiation to see, as at a banquet table, to the correct composition of the carriages, pre-established of course, but many had lost their invitation with their seat number. The convoy set off at last, filling the station with satisfying smoke. The suburbs of the town, the first fields, the entry into the jungle, known as Surprise, in memory of the intrepid gunboat, the track like a long snake weaving through the mass of vegetation...

"Mind the soot!" Casimir warned everybody.

"It smells, in here!" cried Cod's Liver's wife, with her nose in the air.

"The jungle is in a permanent process of decomposition and recomposition," pontificated Amyot, the civil engineer.

"Are we going to see monkeys?" another lady inquired.

"Snakes, raaaather!" hooted someone, no one knew who, in a particularly dark passage of undergrowth.

"And spiders!"

"There you are, I can see one climbing up your skirt," added another joker.

"S'not funny!" spluttered Mrs. Amyot, with her mouth full of biscuits which she had taken with her fearful of being hungry.

To this her husband retorted that he had strongly recommended that she didn't come, or if she did, at least to keep quiet. The Chinese passengers mockingly observed the Whites quarrelling, while feeling out the seats and the partitions of the carriages: were they sufficiently comfortable and safe? After three quarters of an hour, the convoy reached the border. The bunch of customs officers on duty in front of the premises serving as the terminating station, stood to attention while two dozen peasants, brought in from neighbouring villages for effect, welcomed them in their turn with gongs, pipes, fireworks and bravos. Ten minutes later, the train was on its way back to Fort-Bayard.

The same evening, Casimir again treated his railwaymen at Ping's.

"A success, eh, our little venture? You should have seen the looks on the faces of our great travellers… As overawed as kids! Apart from Cod's Liver of course, even more constipated than usual."

Emile and Gabriel were radiant, too:

"We've found a name for the loco."

In France, they had given a name to all their engines. It was a tradition and a proof of affection. The Hohenzollern had proved to be strong, they would pamper her, she would not let them down.

"Very good idea! So, this name?"

"Eliane."

The first name of Emile's mother.

Chapter 11

LÉONIE'S HUSBAND ERNEST came back from work, *L'Equipe* under his arm, a sign that a big sports event, most likely cycling or football, had either just happened or was imminent.

"Roger Rivière tomorrow, at the Vigorelli in Milan, the cycling hour record," he telegraphed to his wife making himself comfortable in his armchair.

"Didn't they tell you anything, at the office?"

As to be expected, he had been told nothing and he knew nothing. Had he found himself in Ménicourt mine the day of the disaster, he would have escaped without even hearing of it.

"Antoinette is dead…"

"Oh merde!"

A cry from the heart, but less intended to sympathize with the fate of the unfortunate than to protest at the obstacle suddenly erected between him and his paper.

"It was murder."

Oh merde! again. But the repeated swearing was perhaps tinged with an awakening of interest in the drama:

"Tell me…"

Léonie did not deviate one iota from the version delivered to Fleurus and the neighbourhood. He sat like an owl dazzled by headlights, but probably only believed the half of this far-too-extraordinary affair, being someone who regarded the mail catalogue of the French Manufacture of Arms and Cycles in Saint-Etienne as a work of science-fiction. Right up to the episode of the Chinese man surprised by their son in the hall of the building. Had

Doctor Gilet diagnosed him with cancer, he would not have felt worse. His wife announced dinner as a means of reinvigoration:

"Tonight, we're having sausage and mash. We're not going to let our appetites be spoiled!"

It didn't quite work though. There was not much enthusiasm for her menu. At table, it was all about the Chinese man. A difficult dish to digest, and, for Frédéric, to describe:

"Small? Tall? Young? Old?"

"Can't remember!"

"Any detail that struck you? His face, his clothes…"

No. The Chinese were people who had neither age nor detail. Frédéric started to perform complicated arabesques with his fork in the mashed potatoes, and Ernest plunged into a silence heavy with reproach; for his wife, his son and both of them together. It was not sufficient that the former discovered Antoinette killed, but on top of that, the latter found himself face to face with the assassin or at the very least a very suspicious character!

"Have you finished?" Léonie asked.

Their plates were still three-quarters full.

"Cheese? Dessert? Nothing else? Shall I clear away?"

She did so. It's then that, loaded with plates, she saw, looking through the window of the lodge, the visage of Belval, the conniving cow from 4th floor, flat A. Already formulating the words to get rid of her: *Ah! Madame Belval, I must admit that it's not the best moment, I still have the bins to clean up, this whole story has made me late…* when she noticed behind the intruder an unknown young man, blond, with a pleasant air about him; a tweed jacket and a polo-neck sweater, modern but without excess, relaxed yet disciplined. Léonie went and dropped her plates in the kitchen, stored away her defensive remarks and came back to open the door for them.

"Madame Burot, I've just learned about the tragedy…"

Two or three grumbles about the difficulties of the times and Belval introduced her companion, who politely had been nodding at each of her comments, but looking as if it did not really agree with them.

"My nephew, Franck."

Although identified as a relative of the cow, this Franck did not lack total sympathy as far as Léonie was concerned. But, as yet she did not understand why he was there…

"Franck is a great reporter with *L'Intransigeant*… It could be interesting for you to talk to him."

The offer intrigued Léonie. The newspapers, they were a universe of their own! And the journalists! They tracked down the secrets of the world.

She invited her visitors to sit down.

"I am off for a walk," mumbled Ernest.

He considered all gentlemen of the press as arrant liars except for those from *L'Equipe*.

Franck Belval cleared his throat.

"First a correction. My aunt always exaggerates. I'm not yet a great reporter, just a trainee."

Belval protested:

"You will be! With all your talent…"

Léonie didn't care. A cub reporter was not so bad. She liked this young, modest man more and more.

"Sorry not to have suggested it earlier, but can I offer you something?"

"Coffee, why not?" Franck accepted.

A sign that he was going to work late. Definitely a remarkable young man. One of those one dreams would make a good son in law, when one has a daughter.

"As for me, if you had a liqueur... Coffee keeps me awake."

On top of her insomnia, Belval complained to anyone ready to hear it about heavy legs, headaches, palpitations and slipped discs, but never anything about her liver.

"Madame Leroux's death reminds me of another drama, which must date back four or five years," started the nephew, once Léonie had put the coffee on and brought out her Cointreau. "The Canut affair. Do you remember?"

No, for the caretaker this news story did not ring a bell.

"Let me tell you... So, Canut, an old sailor, was found at home, in Fécamp, lifeless, a letter in his hands. No mistake as in your case: the envelope, coming from Rio, was definitely addressed to him. The police discovered inside it tiny shards of razor blades impregnated with a rare mixture of curare and other poisons from down there. Canut, not watching, cut himself while tearing open the envelope and succumbed, in indescribable pain. A vengeance, of course. The sailor had in the past lived in Brazil. There he had done a bit of everything, including gold mining with another man called Gervais. Together they ran an enterprise in the forest. They were the best of friends, but you've heard as well as I that gold sends one crazy! Canut, they say cheated Gervais and went back to France rich whereas the other was left there without a penny. Years went by. Revenge is a dish best served cold. Gervais recovered somewhat, built himself another nest egg. Enough to afford the services of a detective in Paris who unearthed Canut, and those of an Indian sorcerer who made the booby-trapped letter. It was the detective who, hearing about Canut's death, understood why Gervais had employed him. He unmasked his employee and the judge had Gervais extradited, and put in jail for thirty years."

The coffee was ready.

"Sugar? Milk?"

No, Franck Belval would drink it black, boiling hot, without anything. A connoisseur.

"You speak of a detective, in your story…" Difficult for Léonie not to draw the analogy between the detective and her son's Chinaman.

"Yes, why?"

"Because I have met the Chinese detective!" proclaimed Frédéric, who had missed nothing of the conversation.

Chapter 12

TWO TRAINS A DAY both ways. Departures at nine a.m. and two p.m. from Fort-Bayard, returns at eleven a.m. and four p.m. from the border. Such was the timetable of the line, posted at the entrance to the station. But the next morning, when they turned up at the depot, very early because they had the idea of painting the name Eliane along the side of the locomotive...

"What are you two doing here?" Pioux shouted at them.

They did not expect to find him there, and even less in this kind of mood. They looked at him, astonished, not understanding. It was as if he reproached them for being there. And since he was staring at them severely without producing any explanation, Gabriel in the end answered that obviously they had come to work.

"Work, what work?"

"What do you mean, what work? What are you talking about? And where is Monsieur Claret-Llobet?"

"Ah, him!"

For several weeks, Vallée and Bouillon found it hard to believe that Casimir had vanished with the cash. They reported to the station every morning, betting on his reappearance, but in the end, they gave up hope. All the evidence, that they had previously refused to see, became painfully obvious. Eliane? Even in handling her most carefully, they would never be able to restore her youth: she was truly at death's door. And the three carriages of the Kowloon Canton Railways Corporation? These, they would have sworn were indestructible. The Chinese workshops to which Casimir had entrusted their repair must have been experts in cosmetics for, shortly afterwards, they fell to pieces; pieces which the people stole under the indifferent eye of the authorities. Very quickly, there was nothing left. On the other hand, the houses and gardens of Fort-Bayard were soon adorned with benches transformed into swing seats, carriage doors enclosing conveniences and panelling erected into fences. The rest of the railway was in the same condition: the rails were rusty, the points were jammed and the station's furniture was worm-eaten… As for the staff; they were short of a dozen employees: tickets sellers, cashiers, conductors and pointsmen, for the railway to function normally.

They consoled themselves by thinking that they were not the only ones to be conned. For the two years that Claret-Llobet had established himself in Fort-Bayard, no one had ever imagined him to be a crook. In fact, was he really one? An entertainer rather, an artist even, in his own way, many thought. After all, he had really built his railway, even if with bits and pieces and with other people's money. All he had done was to leave with the funds necessary for its operation, as if suddenly, tired of his dream, he had wanted to start another somewhere else.

They had been living – "Temporarily, on Casimir's word of honour! Your provided accommodation, right behind the station, will soon be available…" – in two rooms of the superb villa that the authorities had put at the disposal of this now absent gentleman. Of course they had been asked to leave without delay. To go where? To prison, perhaps… For a moment, Ambroggiani, the thick-lipped Corsican with bad breath who was commander of the Indigenous Guard – the police of the territory – almost accused them of complicity with Claret-Llobet:

"Where has he gone? Didn't he tell you of his intentions? His actions never made you suspicious? How did he recruit you? Why did you leave your previous job? How much was he going to pay you?"

How much? An excellent question, that last one. And how? In theory or in practice? Emile and Gabriel had only received a meagre advance on a salary that the sly fox had promised would be tremendous. What they had was not enough to even consider a return trip to France. And indeed, what would they have done there? Who would have taken them back? *Here come the two suckers from the Fort-Bayard railway limping home!* Everyone in Guang-Zhou-Wan already thought of them as such. Soon, all of France, from the Paris-Lyon-Mediterranean line to the Railway of the West, not forgetting their dear Little Belt, would be aware of their misfortune.

The Administrator General, couldn't he see them, offer them some help, a job? Alas! Cod's liver, although so cautious when it came to the train, had – in this Casimir had kept his word – fallen with him. Waiting for his successor, he only dealt with run-of-the-mill, day-to-day affairs. Being linked to the bastard who had deceived the Administration, Bouillon and Vallée were obviously not one of those. The secretary of the recently dismissed A. G. asked them to go and look somewhere else.

Father Cellard, Fort-Bayard's priest, offered them somewhere to sleep in his presbytery, apologizing for the simplicity of the accommodation: "You would be more comfortable at the leprosarium. The sisters of Immaculate Mary have got room…" With the lepers? They already felt like pariahs! The presbytery was more central, more practical, they explained in order to decline the alternative.

"You're looking for a job?" asked the priest.

The question seemed out of place to them. A job? Not here certainly. They went and wandered around the harbour. They would surely find a ship to a place where the scandal had not spread, and for a reasonable price. If needed, they would pay for their passage by working on board... Two weeks later, they were still there. From then on they were spending most of their days along the quays, chatting with the junk owners, eating the two-cent-cuisine of the local restaurants, clinking glasses with toothless, tattooed sailors. Unscrupulous businessmen with cautious sideways glances were willing to place at their disposal ladies or cargoes of all kinds, freight brokers searching for men of straw offered them commissions to front their somewhat opaque transactions.

Each day, too, they passed people even more lost than they: a hairy sage with long nails who was selling his potion of immortality to the crews; an old soldier accompanied by his caged mynah, who had landed here by mistake en route towards his native Shandong which he said he had not seen for thirty years; and a Malay family, the man turbaned, the woman veiled and the children naked, hoping to return to Malacca...

As for them? Macau, Hong Kong, Shanghai, Canton... Not one of these destinations was suitable for them. Too costly, too uncertain, too... in the end, they didn't know any longer. Their willpower grew dim like the waters of the harbour, their energy wore itself out in vain. Two thrushes stuck in glue.

Chapter 13

EIGHT O'CLOCK in the morning. Léonie was cleaning her mirrors in a better mood. She had made a new friend in Franck Belval the evening before. The journalist had succeeded where she and Ernest had failed: in obtaining from Frédéric a description, rather approximate but promising nevertheless, of the Chinese man.

"So you really met a Chinese detective?"

Léonie had wanted to answer in her son's place, to explain to the journalist his fortuitous encounter in the lobby with the mysterious Asian man, but also his unfortunate inability to remember his face.

"Let him speak. I think he knows a lot of things…"

"A detective, yes. With a green anorak, a cap and thick glasses!"

"His height?"

"Like daddy."

"His age?"

"Also like dad."

An anorak in the middle of an Indian summer, a cap and glasses? Accessories of disguise, Belval had analysed. And, who dressed up like that if not detectives? Those of Chinese nationality, in Paris, could not be numerous. Even if Frédéric's detective was not licensed, he could be found. But for all that, Léonie had got a little irritated: "Why on earth didn't you remember all this earlier?" The journalist had advised indulgence: the motivations to a child's recall can be complex. He was right, and in her Frédéric, she knew she had a nice boy. This is what she was thinking about when the face of Fleurus, with a venomous smile on its lips, appeared in the mirror as she wiped away her Windolene. She jumped.

"Did I scare you?"

"No... just surprised."

"Pleasantly, I hope!"

The oafish retort of a cafe waiter.

"Yes, um... you have some news?"

"You have some too, haven't you? Madame Burot, we should talk..."

"Talk? But... about what?"

"Current affairs. Let's go into your lodge."

The inspector opened the latest edition of *L'Intransigeant*. On the front page, François Mitterrand was renewing his appeal for a 'no' at the referendum and Edith Piaf was leaving hospital after her car accident with her current lover, one Georges Moustaki.

"There are lots of things happening in the world, don't you think? But for us, it's on page 2, in the news in brief: 'Paris: Horrific Murder by Poisoned Letter.' Read on!"

She obeyed.

It was yesterday, 19th September, around midday that Léonie Burot, caretaker at number 11, rue François Ponsart, XVIe arrondissement in Paris, made a macabre discovery when taking some milk to her colleague and friend at number 10, Antoinette Leroux. This lady was, in fact, lying stone dead on her kitchen floor. At her feet was a letter addressed to a Jacques Sergent, living at number 11, and probably delivered at number 10 by mistake. Sent from Hong Kong, this unusual post had without doubt aroused Madame Leroux's curiosity, 'almost obsessive since her husband's death' according to Léonie Burot. She actually started to open it, using steam, a well known technique among the indiscreet; a fatal initiative!

Everything leads us to believe that the letter contained a highly toxic substance which, one way or another, killed Antoinette Leroux whose dead body bore the stigmas of a cruel agony: a doubling in size of the tongue and atrocious burns on the face and hands. And the content of this deadly envelope, apart from the poison, the composition of which is still unknown? Some photographs. One of them, showing people and a locomotive in a jungle, had written on the back: 'Eliane, the Surprise, Fort-Bayard, 13th August 1938.' The police, who arrived on the premises shortly after, have expedited an inquiry led by Inspector Félix Fleurus.

Fort-Bayard was the capital of the territory of Guang-Zhou-Wan, a French possession in southern China, not far from Indochina. Jacques Sergent, the addressee of the letter who, without this mistaken delivery, would have opened it and succumbed instead of the victim, has mysteriously disappeared. Nobody knows exactly what this 'levelheaded and polite man,' as his caretaker depicts him, does for a living. 'Still waters run deep' warns the proverb. We can be sure that in the past Jacques Sergent visited Fort-Bayard. What could he have done there to warrant such terrible vengeance? And by whom ? Be that as it may, his elimination had been meticulously prepared, since Léonie Burot's son, Frédéric, ten years old, has confided to us that several weeks before, he had caught sight of a thirty-five year old Chinese man in the building's lobby; a strangely dressed man: 'green anorak, cap and thick glasses'. Was this man a private detective trying to unearth Sergent and sent by the killers? Your dedicated reporter is on his trail, and will not fail to keep you informed of the developments of this dreadful affair.

Franck Belval.

"Madame Burot, understand that I am a little upset."

And what about her, then? Upset? No, outraged, appalled, in pieces!

"The bastard!" she shrieked.

"May I know who you're insulting like this?"

"The journalist, of course! So many lies!"

"Are you trying to tell me that you didn't grant him this interview?" Fleurus said sarcastically.

What? Which interview? With Belval, they had just had a pleasant conversation, without him ever mentioning that he was going to write an article, that same evening, in which moreover he would misquote all her words. Antoinette with *her almost obsessive curiosity since her husband's death!* She had never told him that! At least not in that way. And *Sergent has mysteriously disappeared.* This was too much! She had only repeated to him what she had already confided to Fleurus, and got from Sergent himself: that he had only gone on a brief journey. Last but not least, the journalist was specially quoting Frédéric and his Chinese man. If the latter happened to read the newspapers…

"Rightly so! This story, why didn't you mention it to me?"

"Because at the time I didn't know anything about it!"

Was it so difficult to understand? The inspector had arrived at one o'clock, gone at two. Frédéric had classes until four-thirty.

"You will protect him, won't you?"

Léonie's eyes were becoming misty with tears.

"All right, all right, don't panic…"

Salsify looked like he could start singing *Tout va très bien Madame la Marquise* (All is well your Ladyship).

"Put yourself in my place…"

"OK… Which school does your boy go to?"

"Rue des Bauches."

"May I make a phone call?"

She showed him the phone.

"Hello, Brissac? It's Fleurus. Who is available…? Verger? Send him to the boys' school at rue des Bauches, in Passy. Tell him to keep an eye out, and if he spots a Chink nosing about, he is not to let him go… Yes, it's to do with the Leroux case."

Salsify hung up.

"Feeling better?"

Léonie sniffed a yes. Fleurus then, with a sleight of hand a magician would envy, replaced the newspaper with a hardback file, somewhat worn.

"Earlier on you asked me if I had any news. I have… The pictures. The letter contained eight more. Here are the enlargements. Have a look…"

On the first four there appeared the same people: the two white men, the big lady, also white, and the young Chinese girl; still in the jungle, in front of the locomotive, in slightly different poses. On the fifth and sixth photos, a new comer had replaced the moustached European: a Chinese adolescent pulling faces, like a monkey, hanging onto the clothes of the lady old Joubert had called the fat white lump. The last two photographs featured the second white man waving from the cabin of the locomotive; but the venue was not the jungle anymore, more a kind of workshop.

"The note on the back of these pictures is different: 'Gabriel and Eliane at the depot, FB, Nov. 36.'"

"Eliane, that would be the locomotive then?"

"It seems so. And this chap inside it, Gabriel. Do any of these people mean any more to you than they did yesterday?"

"No… but Fort-Bayard, it's really in China?"

In the catalogue of allegations proffered by Belval, this at least seemed true. But Léonie had never heard of such a place.

"At the office, nobody knew it either," Salsify reassured her. "Even our archivist placed it somewhere near Madagascar."

Chapter 14

"YOU ARE FRENCH train drivers?" a nasal voice with a local accent shouted at them, on their umpteenth morning at the port. They turned round. A rather scruffy Chinese adolescent was staring mischievously at them, like an impish young fox.

"Me Wawa!"

"Where did you learn French?"

"Me no learn!"

They soon found out, with Wawa it was the school of the streets, fixing things and helping out foreigners in all kinds of ways; in the end, he managed the language better than the rich kids who went to the Friars' College.

"Me like trains!" he announced very keenly.

This declaration was enough to bond them.

"Me see you at port often. You look for junk?"

They admitted they were looking, but apparently not in the sense understood by Wawa.

"My father has shop for boats, there, close by," he said pointing to a shop with a mishmash of boating components spilling out onto the quay. "He has beautiful junk at Pointe Nivet also. You sleep there if you want. Him very happy!"

They answered that they would not want to disturb, but deep inside they were immediately tempted by the offer: to stay on a boat moored on the edge of the territory sounded to their ears almost like the departure they had given up hoping for. That very evening they met on the junk. Beautiful, as Wawa had promised? Not quite; humid, rattling, breaking up, patched up and full of putrid smells.

But Pointe Nivet, a tiny peninsula on which stood a fishing hamlet and where people could not care in the least about the 'suckers from the railway', exuded pretty much the charm of a haven.

Wawa and his parent welcomed them with some rice wine which they drank while contemplating the peaceful village outlined by the moonlight. The father offered to sell them a set of anchors, a boat engine, a trawl net and even a flock of goats.

"We don't have any money," they replied to each proposition, which did not prevent the next one following.

"You poor? You do same everybody here: you smuggle!" explained Wawa.

Calculating that after fifteen days, they would not have a *sapèque* left in their pockets, they considered the suggestion quite seriously. Smuggling, why not, but…

"Smuggling what?"

"Everything: guns, machinery, alcohol, opium… Easy!"

Easy when one is drunk. The next morning, they were above all concerned with getting rid of their headaches and stiffness from the night spent on the hard beds of the old tub.

Chapter 15

FLEURUS CALLED IN again at the beginning of the afternoon.

"I've got the results of the tests."

"The tests…" echoed Léonie in a toneless voice.

"Yes. It must seem very quick to you. Usually, in the department, if we have something to get our teeth into after a week, we can consider ourselves lucky. But this time, I don't know why, perhaps the bizarre nature of the case… Beaumont, the forensic pathologist, was as excited as a child."

Léonie muttered "Good," but meant "Bad." Wouldn't the problems now start?

"Alas, I must confirm what the journalist wrote in his paper: your friend was murdered…"

She sighed audibly to express her condemnation of the crime.

"You remember the oily layer and the small brownish stains on the back of the first photo?"

Léonie grunted again, regretfully affirmative, while Salsify was unfolding a typed document.

"The doc's note. In short…

A complex mixture… Three essential components.

1st. Lewisite: a toxic agent derived from arsenic, concocted during the Great War – same type as mustard gas, but acting more rapidly – contamination by absorption through the skin or lungs – provokes burns, erythema and blisters on the infected surfaces + destroys the pulmonary system;

2nd. Gelatin: lewisite is viscous in its natural form – the

79

gelatin contributes to its solidification;

3rd. Etorphine: alkaloid similar to morphine but more violent – mixed with the molecules of lewisite penetrating through the skin, reinforced their toxic effect and provoked a lethal catatonia...

There you are. All the photos were soaked with this cocktail. For your information, Beaumont has added:

a) Lewisite today forbidden or very much controlled (military) – but common knowledge that the Japanese used it in China – still probable illegal stocks over there;

b) Etorphine is a derivative of opium, for which Hong Kong remains a nerve centre;

c) Only a very good chemist would be able to put together such a poison;

d) The gelatin stabilizes the lewisite but reduces its penetrating power..."

The inspector paused theatrically before resuming:

"There's a snag here..."

Léonie startled out of her reverie, opened her eyes wide.

"It's simple. According to Beaumont, the gelatin restrains the lewisite. If Sergent himself had opened his letter in normal conditions, some foul toxins would certainly have penetrated his body sufficiently to choke and partly paralyze him, but not enough to cause his death, especially not instantaneously..."

"But, Antoinette?"

"The steam, Madame Burot, the steam to unseal the letter! It melted the gelatin and released the lewisite at the same time as the other nasty stuff, the etorphine. Your friend breathed in the whole lot; that's what the autopsy revealed..."

Léonie winced: Antoinette on a police slab, all cut up, her lungs opened up, eaten into by the poison, blue, revolting, like the calfs' lungs she sees in the market.

"Anyway, without wanting to be unpleasant, I would say that Madame Leroux perished as the victim of her misplaced curiosity."

Fleurus's statement was like the performance of a clumsy knife thrower. Pierced to her heart, the caretaker tried to recall the past days and run through the events, from the arrival of the postman that morning up to Antoinette's collapse. Alas! The postman did indeed come and had indeed given her the letter, she had indeed looked at it carefully, found it strange, and had indeed visited her colleague... *Do you want to open it?* What had her reply been? Some hypocrisy, some cowardliness. She thought herself monstrous.

Chapter 16

HENRIETTE VALLÉE was supposed to join her husband, between six to eight months after he arrived, the happy couple had agreed, giving him time to settle in properly and her to straighten out their affairs in France. The day after his arrival in Fort-Bayard, Gabriel had sent his dearly beloved a long and passionate letter about his new job. Afterwards, he had not dared to write to her again. She showed up at the junk one morning, much earlier than planned, driven by Wawa who had picked her up at the arrival of the *Hué*.

"Me understand quick: your wife!"

Vallée was not a small person, but next to his Henriette… "My queen, my mare, my better half yet my double!" Gabriel had more than once painted pictures of her ample proportions to the young Chinese, who had been favourably impressed by them.

"Don't say anything, I know everything, I learnt of it from the newspapers. That man, what a bastard!"

Her husband was in the middle of shaving. He threw himself, with foam and tears on his face, into the well padded arms of his spouse. Emile and Wawa were moved. Henriette glared at them; they beat a hasty retreat.

When they reappeared, two hours later:

"We are going to open a café, even a café-restaurant!"

"We'll do accommodation, as well. It's non-existent here; look at where you two are staying."

"My little wife, she's always full of good ideas."

"And always with a little in reserve. I have a small sum from my late father; I'll break open my cashbox and we can start. Without being immodest, I think I can accomplish wonderful things. Gabriel's misfortune has become the chance of our lives!"

The misfortunate changed the subject:

"Yes, well er… you, Wawa… we thought of…"

"Employing you as waiter," cut in Henriette.

"Yes, that's it, waiter. Well, you could be a handy man, do a bit of everything; the washing-up, the cleaning, the shopping… Would you like that?"

The teenager quivered with impatience. Of course he would like that. So close to Madame Vallée! She passed an affectionate hand through his hair, and Gabriel proposed to bring out a bottle of wine from 'the wine cellar on the junk'.

"And you, old friend?" he turned to Emile, suddenly realizing that his comrade had been left out of the plan. "How about you becoming our associate?"

"You know very well that I haven't got a bean."

"Bah! Work can also be regarded as Capital," retorted Gabriel who had in the past attended a course in economy and politics organized by the transport unions.

"I'll think about it."

"I hope so!"

All said in a tone leaving no doubt whatsoever that both of them had already put the eventuality into the domain of dreams.

Chapter 17

S CHOOL COMES OUT again, Léonie picks up Frédéric, they return home, mother on the lookout, child, as proud as a peacock.

"Hey! Madame Burot!"

The caretaker jumped at the voice though it was already familiar. Fleurus and a colleague with the large nose of a lover of strong drinks, in his late fifties, were coming up behind them quickly.

"Verger, my colleague," Fleurus introduced him when they caught up. "He is going to ensure the protection of your son to whom, as I told you, I must speak. We'll see you home."

Léonie resigned herself, but stated her conditions:

"You'll have to be a little patient with your questions. My little one is not used to this. First his tea; he must keep his strength up."

Salsify refused the glass of beer offered by Léonie: never any alcohol whilst on duty. Verger, although tempted, followed suit in this cardinal... and statutory... virtue. They waited, quietly, around the table of the lodge, until Frédéric finished up his chocolate-spread sandwich and his squash.

"All right, some time ago you saw a Chinese man writing down the names of the people in the building," once tea had been gulped down Fleurus could at last start.

Frédéric confirmed, with a large chocolate smile for Verger, who was encouraging him by pulling faces.

"Now I'd like you to look at some pictures; photos of Chinese bandits."

"Eh! Oh! Just a minute!" interrupted Léonie. "There was never any talk of showing such ruffians to my son. Won't he have nightmares about them?"

"It's imperative that he looks at them," Fleurus insisted.

And addressing Frédéric again:

"Perhaps the faces of one or two of them will remind you of your Chinaman. You understand?"

The child eagerly grabbed the pack of portraits.

Léonie was uneasy about the sinister faces which the police imposed on her son: tattooed, one-eyed and scarred, to say nothing of one that was missing one ear and both nostrils. But far from frightening Frédéric, these hideous rogues prompted him and the old policeman to have a good laugh during which the portraits, one after the other, were likened to porcupines, cockroaches and weasels.

"Will you stop distracting the kid!" said Fleurus, irritated and concerned about maintaining some semblance of seriousness to the interview.

"But he is the one who is making all this up!" protested Verger still falling about.

Without warning, Fleurus suddenly took away his photographs of yellow crooks, and replaced them with the enlargements of Fort-Bayard. Not much chance that the picnickers would arouse any memories from the young boy but at least, apart from the gigantic white woman, they would not give rise to amusement.

"And here, do you recognize anyone?"

"Yes! My Chinese!"

Frédéric pressed his finger on the adolescent whose contortions were making the obese lady laugh.

"But… Didn't you tell the journalist that he was the same age as your daddy?"

"It's still him, all the same."

"The photograph is from 1938," his mother intervened pinching her son's cheek affectionately to congratulate him.

Chapter 18

THE TRAVELLERS, the Vallées' café-hotel-restaurant, opened on May 1st. One could see the sea from the first floor, on a clear day. A rare phenomenon, but as Gabriel professed, at his sparkling new beer pump provided by the Brasseries et Glacières de l'Indochine: "You can also find sun in our hearts."

The Travellers quickly established its clientele, local for the bar and the restaurant, foreign for the hotel: a number of faithful customers staying briefly but regularly in Fort-Bayard made it one of their habits. The maverick preacher Owens who, to the great displeasure of Father Cellard, came from Hong Kong to convert the natives replete with baubles and beads, swore by the owner's wine and room number two. There was also Szeckti, an Austro-Hungarian citizen who pretended to be an artist selling his wares but who was certainly trading something more exciting; Ambroggiani had his eye on him. He sometimes stayed five or six days in a row. But this was nothing compared to the Oliveira brothers. These twins, traders in fashion from Macau, with a funereal air about them, appeared every month to present to the ladies of the territory their most beautiful models of dresses, shoes and hats. They rented three rooms, two to sleep in and one to display their collections. They livened up the place very much with people flocking to stare at the procession of customers who, with dignity, went upstairs with the brothers to stifled laughter at the bar…

"Gentlemen don't be mistaken, the house is respectable!" protested Henriette.

The Vallées radiated a joy which Emile judged vulgar and a little harsh. To compensate for his not joining them in their business – he had once and for all declined their offer – they had proposed to lodge him.

"I wouldn't want to disturb your operations…"

He stayed on the junk of Pointe Nivet. Wawa came to see him every day before work, badgering him on the propositions of easy money which he no longer listened to.

"You think about it. Me come back tomorrow."

"Yeh, right, see you tomorrow."

He would go back to sleep or brooded over his fate. On one of these gloomy mornings, as the youth had just left him…

"Good morning, may I…?"

On top of the ladder leading to the cabin, a man he had never seen before was holding onto the handrail.

"My name is Edmond Leblanc. I am the director of Customs and Excise of Fort-Bayard…"

Bouillon let his visitor descend and asked him without conviction to sit down.

"What is it about?"

"I've learned about your misfortune… the railway…" Leblanc was appalled. Who could one trust nowadays? However…

"I cannot say without impropriety that your troubles delight me. Yet… One of my assistants has unexpectedly died. The officer who collects the tax which pays for the collection of statistics. May he rest in peace, but this death has taken us by surprise, at a time when we are a little busy… In short, I'm looking for a replacement for To."

"To?"

"Yes, my late employee. I forgot to tell you… The job of assistant usually is assigned to indigenous people of

90

Indochina. But of course a French person can apply, if he is not offended by the offer. Railwaymen have a reputation of being very resourceful. You would be a choice recruit and quickly promoted. Are you tempted?"

"The thing is…"

Occupying the post of an Annamite did not overly shock Bouillon. On the other hand, would it be right for a railwayman to become an agent of Customs and Excise, responsible for collecting a tax which might bring in ten francs a year? Was it not demeaning himself in the same way that Gabriel did with his bar?

"I should normally follow the usual procedure and go through my superior who would send someone from Hanoi… taking six months in the best-case scenario. I can't postpone for so long. There exists an emergency recruiting system. I'll invoke that and will plead the higher interest of the service in order to employ you without delay…"

Procedure, superiors, service… By using this administrative language, Leblanc's tone had become firmer, his delivery accelerated. One felt he was on his home ground.

"Rest assured, I'll brief you. It's not complicated."

Of this, Emile had no doubt. A month later, he and the Customs and Excise Director went to see Cod's Liver's replacement, whose department was supposed to back the nomination of any new employee. The man, cheerful, good natured and with an over abundance of aftershave, had already been given the nickname: Eau de Cologne. He eulogized the job of statistics-tax collection:

"It symbolizes that Guang-Zhou-Wan is not, contrary to what our enemies want people to believe, a den of smugglers but a fundamental cog in the commerce of the region. So, Monsieur Bouillon, there is no such thing as a worthless profession. You won't regret your decision!"

Chapter 19

"HE DID IT! Roger Rivière just beat the world hour record. Even with a puncture."

Ernest did not expand on the champion's achievement. A colleague had lent him *L'Intransigeant* which he waved under his wife's nose.

"And blah blah blah…"

Léonie did not want to get into that argument:

"Our Frédéric has recognized the Chinese. He pointed him out to the police, in the pictures they had brought with them this afternoon."

"Bloody hell! And you are jubilant about it?"

Wasn't this a good opportunity to acknowledge proof of their son's intelligence? And wasn't it an invaluable step forward in the enquiry?

"God! You're worse than irresponsible! Here you go again! Vultures like your journalist, there are hundreds of them, thousands. I bet that within twenty-four hours, they'll all be writing about it. Huge headlines: 'Criminal Identified by Caretaker's Son!' Maybe they'll even publish his photograph and our address!"

"No, they wouldn't dare, and the police would protect us," Léonie retorted thinking that yes, Belval and his colleagues would dare, and that the protection offered by the forces of the law was today embodied in a frivolous, and probably alcoholic, old man.

"I won't be fooled again. I won't talk to the press anymore."

Her ultimate defence, and the strongest after all.

"Haven't you understood yet that with reporters,

answering or not is all the same? They're the experts at making up stories! I tell you, we'll soon see them and the damage they cause…"

The phone rang.

"Aha! And so it begins. God save us from those hacks!"

Léonie went to answer with other expectations in mind. Only the residents of the building had her number. In fact it was they who had decided, in a general meeting, to equip the lodge with a phone. For their personal convenience mainly: at the blowing of the smallest fuse, the blockage of the washing basin, they didn't bother to go downstairs, they picked up the phone. She herself didn't use it much. "Be careful not to overuse it, the calls outside Paris will be charged to you," the chairman of the residents' committee had warned her, as undiplomatic as it was vain. Who on earth could she have called? No one in her family in the Loiret owned the Bakelite device yet.

"Hello? Good evening Madame Burot. Can you talk?" said a voice from the telephone.

At first she did not understand the question, nor the identity of the person who posed it.

"… This is Monsieur Sergent. Am I disturbing you?"

"Not at all."

Disturbing her? Certainly not! With his call Sergent was perhaps going to turn her life upside down, but she did not really want to say that.

"I read the newspapers," he continued. "I'm deeply saddened about Madame Leroux. And I'm bringing trouble to you too. Please forgive me…"

He spoke with a halting delivery which she didn't know he had.

She would have liked to interrupt him, comfort him with kind words. He did not give her time.

"I can't come home… they're hunting me…"

The confession of an animal brought to bay.

"Where are you?"

"I'd prefer not to tell you…"

A silence, then Sergent spoke again:

"Without wanting to embarrass you… would you be prepared to do me a small service?"

"Ask me, feel free." In the same tone as she would have used to encourage him to ask her to iron his shirts.

"It's a delicate matter but I have to ask… I may be in need of a bit of money."

A strangled astonishment remained stuck in Léonie's throat. Lending money to Sergent? Considering what she earned, such a gesture was not really on the cards. She would of course have to consult Ernest who would take her for… she did not dare to imagine what.

"You have probably already seen the little safe that I have at home, in my office," the fugitive went on.

"Ah, yes of course!"

The caretaker was relieved and at the same time slightly ashamed to have been thinking at cross purposes. Sergent, of course, was not the kind of man to cadge from his peers. But what she now imagined his intention to be, wasn't that just as extraordinary?

"This safe, I keep some savings in it. If I were to give you the combination, you could withdraw the contents, then we could meet in a safe location. Would this be acceptable?"

"Yes."

Her own answer amazed her. She was forced to be concise in front of Ernest and Frédéric, but couldn't she have nuanced her intonation, tempered her reply or expressed some reserve…?

"Thank you with all my heart… I will make it up to you."

"Not necessary…"

"I insist. Can I call you again tomorrow, same time, to give you the combination and arrange a rendezvous?"

"Ok."

"So, I'll talk to you tomorrow. One last point… It would be better not to mention this conversation to the police. They would misunderstand."

Of course she was not going to whistle any tune of money smuggling to the police at the Quai des Orfèvres. Nor at home…

"It was Monsieur Sergent. He wanted to apologize for the trouble he is causing us and to say hello. He is all right," she summed up for her husband and her son when she had hung up.

"Is that all?" asked Ernest a bit suspiciously.

"No. He said he won't be coming back just yet."

"For all we care! Why doesn't he whinge directly to the police? Who does he think we are, the Salvation Army?"

Chapter 20

THE VALLÉES SEEMED even more overjoyed than Emile about his new job.

"Let's celebrate!" Gabriel decided.

"Yes," approved Henriette. "Tonight we'll close the place and keep it just for us. My friend, I shall prepare an exquisite feast for your delectation."

It was not ten o'clock and they were already drunk, especially the hostess who loved wine more than it did her.

"Gentlemen, I'm off to bed…"

The departure of Madame Vallée had a strange effect on Wawa. As if a party without her was not a party anymore. All the same, his agile mind never left him short of ideas. Despite his young age, he knew all the brothels in the territory well. One in particular was managed by his aunt.

"If you want, we go there," he suggested. "Many pretty girls, and aunty give us good price!"

Emile and Gabriel hesitated. Henriette had gone to bed without any inkling…

"… We just look. Aunty very funny, very nice."

'Closed place where there is voluptuous' – Wawa's translation – was located past Pointe Nivet, in a rather special zone: one did not exactly know whether it was part of Guang-Zhou-Wan or not for, by some unlikely chance, the territory conquered by the French was somehow geometrically flexible. During the negotiations, the French Navy had said to the Chinese: "No final limits to our colony until we have been able to explore in our own good time," which meant, *get out quickly and let us occupy the place.* The Mandarins, cleverly, had agreed to that: "No problem.

Here, you're at home!" The Treaty of the Cession of Guang-Zhou-Wan had consequently drawn the border very roughly and had referred its final boundary markings to a joint commission at a future date. This group had met two or three times, enough for each side to realise its disagreement with the other. Forty years later, the colony still did not have officially established contours and the Chinese turned around their initial words, as soon as the French interfered in the contested areas: "Sorry Gentlemen, here, we're at home." Guang-Zhou-Wan was then filled with enclaves of uncertain status. Wawa's aunt and other smart people had understood that settling there, under the two disputing States, would result in fiscal rule and public order enforcement... by neither.

In the brothel's salon full of darkened corners, prevailed a twilight, cleverly emitted by small red and yellow rice paper lanterns inside which spicy perfumed candles were burning. The furniture, a combination of eras and styles – Chinese, European and even Siamese and Javanese – seemed to have been arranged haphazardly, like a collection of theatre props. The madam, overly made up, was lazing on soft cushions on a sofa. About ten girls were standing in the background. Bouillon saw one only, an adolescent with a face as pale as the moon which sent shivers down his spine. He avoided her look, full of severity, and very quickly, almost at random, chose another girl, an impudent one who giggled as he followed her upstairs. When they came down again, 'Pale-moon face' had disappeared. He could not bear the idea that she was busy with another client. He prevailed on his companions to leave the premises with him.

The next day, he asked Wawa: "What was the name of

the very young one? The one who… I mean… she was standing on the right hand side."

"Pah?"

To Emile, this name seemed perfect.

"Where is she from?"

"Me not sure: Lei-Zhou, Guang-Xi… Father, mother dead, she kidnapped by pirates. Auntie buy her. All girls here like this, or sell by parents."

A slave, in other words. What's eating you, Bouillon?

One week later…

"I'd like to buy Pah."

"For marriage?"

The Frenchman sidestepped the question. Did he even know what was motivating him? Desire? The wish to accomplish a good act? The jealousy and disgust of knowing she is being soiled by other men? The will to relieve his solitude? A bit of everything no doubt, but he had not given it a lot of thought. Had he done so, would he have changed his mind?

"Ask your aunt how much she wants for her."

More than his wages for a month. He did not have such a sum.

"My uncle lend you the money."

Once the loan was concluded they went back to the brothel one lunch time. Pah was waiting, all ready to go, in the middle of the lounge which was gloomy without its lights.

"Here merchandise! Good quality!" Wawa praised her.

When they walked out of the house, Emile noticed that his acquisition was limping slightly. The young girl smiled at him awkwardly, as if to apologize, and so revealed two gold front teeth.

"This nothing!" Wawa reassured him.

The teenager had only been hit accidentally with a scythe while working in the fields. As for the teeth, he did not know why, but he thought that the alternating colours of gold and ivory were very smart.

Bouillon took Pah to The Travellers where he knew he would find the Oliveira brothers. She gently fingered the clothes which the Portuguese presented, with the strange and fragile tenderness of a wild animal which remains docile as long as it does not hear the call of the wild. Emile decided for her and treated her to a bright yellow dress as well as a pair of blue slippers trimmed with a silver thread which brought out the somewhat backhanded compliment:

"Your feet look just like a flower garden!"

On the way back, she started to sing. Was it her way of saying thank you to him?

Chapter 21

ANTOINETTE'S FUNERAL took place in Saint-Ouen, in the northern suburbs of Paris. In the church, Léonie intoned along with the Requiem with some enthusiasm. After the service, the tiny cortege, about ten people, followed the hearse to the cemetery. There, astonishment. There were other parishioners, whom she would have preferred not to see, waiting around the grave where Antoinette would rejoin her husband: lover Dédé and his mate Philibert, plus the betrayer Franck Belval who gave her a wink which she did not appreciate. Who did he think he was? With an annoyed grimace, she tried to keep him at a distance, but the Judas approached her anyway. The worst thing was that he seemed rather pleased with himself for having displayed his prowess at informing the public with his article. Maybe he was even expecting her to thank him for having pulled her out of anonymity.

"You know what they say about murderers and the final resting place of their victim," he murmured. "I'm keeping watch…"

Léonie could not stop herself taking a look around them, which delighted him. She could have slapped his face! Fortunately, he walked away. And now Dédé and Philibert, in their turn, approached her. What ill wind was driving them?

"Sad, eh?" said the former. "When I think, I was supposed to see her on that day… But something came up… Destiny eh!"

"I read the article about you in *L'Intransigeant*," added the latter. "It was first-rate."

God! Make me deaf rather than have me listen to the follies of these two good-for-nothings. Perhaps they had only come here on the look out for new catches. There! Weren't they ogling one of Antoinette's cousins just a little too long? The stupid goose did not look put out either. She was smiling back at Dédé from underneath her black veil.

A branch of the box tree was passed from hand to hand to allow everyone to bless the coffin, then the condolences, the grave covered… and then this moment when one does not know what to do; leave, stay a while or chat with the others to see what their plans are.

"You're going home?"

It was Philibert who was at it again, alone: Dédé had vanished, the cousin too.

"Can I take you back? I have my car…"

And she her bus, which would take her back to Passy just as quickly and in much better company!

"Oh! Shall I give you my phone number, then?"

The cold silence that followed convinced him not to persevere; he walked away. *With his tail between his legs, being the appropriate expression!* she said to herself, laughing and watching him leave, silly and contrite just like an anteater deprived of ants. She too left the cemetery and went to the bus stop. *With his tail between his legs…* that joke Antoinette would have understood straight away: *I laughed so much, I wet my pants!* God. Léonie's face darkened. What is this life, this death? One moment you laugh, the next you cry… And this bus, where is it? She looked at the crossroads at the bottom of the street, her hand shading her eyes from the sun.

My Goodness! Aren't some people odd?

A dark haired woman wrapped up in an over large, heavy, winter coat when the temperature must have been around 20 degrees Celsius was holding a bouquet tight against her chest and hobbling along in her direction. Reaching Léonie, she lifted her head…

Mother of God!

Twenty years older, as with her son's detective, but the same mouth sewn with a silk thread, the same tiny figurine look: the Chinese girl in the photos! Léonie immediately started to follow her. The Asian woman turned in the direction of the cemetery and reached the gate. A pause to check that there was no one inside, and she entered. Wandering through the rows, she was looking for a specific grave. Antoinette's. When she found it she laid her flowers, which Léonie, hidden behind a tomb twenty meters away, could see better now. They were not the type that one takes to a funeral. The lilac-purple petals swayed graciously on long stems shooting out of a nest of pulpy leaves and aerial roots which were curling like the fancy knot on a gift-wrapped purchase. Léonie had already seen some, illustrated in *Le Jardin des Modes*, old copies of which the Baroness de La Brosse had given her. They were orchids.

"And now, what do you think is going to happen?"

Who was this? That fathead Philibert still wandering about? She turned briskly, ready to push him out of the way. Wrong! It was Franck Belval.

"… Didn't I tell you that murderers always come back to their victims' final resting place?"

He put his index finger to his lips, winked again at her, pulled out a camera from under his jacket and, stepping into the alley, focused.

"Mademoiselle! Beware!"

Without hesitation, Léonie tackled the journalist with all the vigour of a second row forward. They rolled onto the ground, while a shadow jumped above their entwined bodies: the Chinese woman, who was running at full tilt despite her limp. Léonie, knees and elbows scratched, slowly stood up. Lying on the ground, a trickle of blood on his forehead, his camera smashed beside him, Franck Belval was groaning, unable to get up.

Chapter 22

HIS COLLEAGUES, ten or so Annamites trained in the colleges of Hanoi, would not have stood out in the sub-prefecture of Bayeux or Argentan in France. Emile was not trying to distinguish himself from them, since the keeping of the tax register required nothing more than his application to a dull and boring routine. However they clearly kept him out of their circle; he was not one of them.

He was not at all distressed about this ostracism. In any case, he reported to Leblanc only, wondering sometimes if the latter had recruited him simply to have a fellow countryman with him and to feel less isolated. His boss, still young, occasionally confided to him some fragments of his professional life: the Colonial School, a first post in Vinh then a position at the department of the Resident General in Tonkin...

"A cocoon. I wanted to leave, get some experience in the field. The post of Director of Customs and Excise in Fort-Bayard was vacant. I applied..." Wasn't Leblanc one of a large family of dreamers? As for the field, in Fort-Bayard he rarely set foot in it, and he boasted with a sometimes disarming naivety about the sacrosanct objectives of his Mission. All of a sudden, he would start something. He would summon his employees and solemnly explain to them how important it was that they rigorously and assiduously applied themselves to their tasks, including, and above all, the refinement of opium, in the famous 'distillery' which Emile and Gabriel had thought, when they first arrived, was dedicated to the production of alcohol. This activity was very lucrative, but was becoming something of a divisive issue. France, signatory of international treaties drastically limiting the drugs trade, exempted itself from such restrictions in its colonies. The French were reviled more and more harshly for this.

"Unfair! We know very well that the product is not for everyone. Therefore in Indochina for a long time we have entrusted its management to Customs and Excise."

Who is *We*?

"The great Paul Doumer."

And a *long time*?

"Since 1901," Leblanc usually added, to give his words an undeniable and apparently incontestable authority. The employees nodded vigorously. A real session of gymnastics which spurred on the fervour of the speaker.

In Fort-Bayard, the refinery operated only to satisfy the needs of the local clientele. China had prohibited the drug since the establishment of the Republic so it was out of the question to sell there. But because everyone seemed to have heard, from here and there, that the contrary was true, Leblanc made the first concession: "I willingly recognize some mistakes were made in the past when our predecessors, in order to face the increasing demand, had to come up with an alternative to the monopoly. I am talking about production under a license which, in the beginning, anybody could buy: the widow Madame Bertrand, the mandarin Monsieur Kouei, the average Mr. So-and-So…" Private refineries had proliferated, inspiring a boom in trafficking. The Administration had had to clean things up: "No more than four licenses for the whole of Guang-Zhou-Wan!" This soon gave rise to another type of excess: the four licensed refineries, although theoretically restricted to quotas, became powerful enterprises, too powerful at times. "In short, the Service was yet again losing control…"

Dismayed faces in the audience, who had however sufficiently suckled at the teats of Chinese philosophy to know they need not be too anxious: for a person who declines, grows again, one who drops to the bottom of a lake, can only come up.

"The scandal of the *Wing On* has opened our minds…" Leblanc feasted on the incredible story of this bulk carrier plying between Fort-Bayard and Macau, which was inspected out at sea one day by the Chinese Customs. A routine inspection, but the Celestial Kingdom's customs duties collectors discovered her hold was packed with opium from French Customs and Excise. The captain then produced some export and import certificates, duly stamped by the relevant administrations. These documents attested the opium came indeed from Fort-Bayard, and more specifically from the Seng refinery, the largest of the four. It was to be delivered to the Tax-Farm of Macau, an institution overseeing the distribution of all strategic merchandise throughout the Portuguese colony. In such circumstances, the Chinese customs officers cannot say anything. Nevertheless, they are puzzled. France asserts that its policy is not to export its opium. Portugal, just as firmly, guarantees importing it in small quantities only, and then exclusively from Goa.

Have the two countries changed their stance? asks Peking. No! reply Paris and Lisbon, there does not exist any opium trade between Fort-Bayard and Macau. What about the official documents found on the *Wing On* then?

"Fake!" said Leblanc indignantly. The French have ordered an inquiry. It shines a light onto the criminal activities of the Seng refinery. The owner, Seng Loon-Fat, nicknamed The Lobster because of his protruding eyes and excessively red hands, like the crustacean's pincers – the result of a scalding in his youth, so the rumour goes, by a jealous husband on whose wife he had dared to put them – has illegally imported stocks of raw opium from Guizhou province, and clandestinely doubled his refinement capacity. Where could one offload this illegal surplus? Difficult in Fort-Bayard. On the other hand, Macau accommodates numerous opium dens. A profitable market which one should only penetrate with a feigned respect for forms and legality. The Lobster admits: he is the one who stole the headed paper and the chops from the administrations in Fort-Bayard and Macau in order to establish the fake covering documents. All the Macau clients had to do to receive the opium, was to pretend they were the representatives of the Tax Farm, more easily-falsified documents, if indeed they needed them: "Methinks these clowns never had to pretend they were anyone other than themselves: Dos Santos and Company!" By stating this Leblanc was passing on a theory well spread among the French: Dos Santos, the Tax Farmer General of Macau, had been, with the Lobster, the instigator of all this trafficking. Therefore Leblanc did not like him.

"Let's avoid dealing with him on principle. And if we can't do otherwise, let's be extremely vigilant," for the Lusitanian was still trading. He had even recently made an official visit to Guang-Zhou-Wan. His flabby jowls covered with a growth of reddish hair made him look like a devious guinea pig. No one had found him likeable.

However that might have been, the *Wing On* affair had signed the death warrant of the system of the four licenses.

"Long live, once more, the one refinery!" It alone,

maintained Leblanc, allowed the healthy, non speculative and transparent business of opium production in Fort-Bayard. The fact that the amount produced, in relation to the population, showed a proportion of consumption per head sufficient to slay three generations in one go – women and children included – hardly bothered him: "You know very well that people stock up. Quite apart from the fact that between the refining and the distribution, there are considerable losses." In actual fact his goal, in the years to come, was to reduce these losses.

Chapter 23

"NOTHING SENSATIONAL in the news today, but doubtless tomorrow, the saga will continue with yet another significant event," Fleurus almost sneered, *L'Intransigeant* held aloft like a flaming torch.

One could tell he had prepared his phrase well in advance.

"Will it be to do with Monsieur Belval?"

"Unless you knocked out somebody else…"

Did Salsify think he was funny? He sniggered before getting a grip on himself, suddenly concentrated and serious:

"Right, let's sum up. This morning, after the funeral, in circumstances which I still find obscure, you spot a Chinese woman who is spending a moment of silence at Antoinette Leroux's graveside. You decide to keep watch on her. Next to you is Franck Belval, with his camera…"

Léonie gently nodded her head.

"This Chinese lady is probably a crucial witness in the murder of your colleague…"

More silent agreement.

"And, the moment Belval tries to take a picture of her, you scream 'Lookout miss!' and you throw yourself on top of him."

"That's right."

"But… tell me… you… er…"

Precursory hesitations to an affront.

"Haven't you thought for one minute of putting the interests of the inquiry before your personal feelings of resentment?"

"I admit I haven't."

"You admit that you haven't! With all due respect, Madame Burot, perhaps the events of these last few days have, if you'll allow me, hit you harder than you realise?"

"I'll pay for Monsieur Belval's medical care," said Léonie evading the question.

"Well. I hope you have good insurance, because the bill is going to be steep. Cranial trauma, dislocation of the shoulder and a broken arm, you really gave him a good going over. Without mentioning his camera: now only good for the breaker's yard and apparently it cost a fortune…"

"Is he going to prosecute me? Are you going to put me in jail?"

Léonie suddenly wanted to know everything about her case, just like a patient who kept her eyes closed to a disease for too long. Fleurus shrugged his shoulders.

"You will know soon enough. Above all I think that Belval too wonders if you're not a bit…"

"Deranged? Then it'll be the asylum…"

"Stop talking nonsense!"

The policeman's face reddened with irritation. Strangely enough, because of that, he was becoming more affable.

"I won't go inside, then?"

Salsify kicked that ball into touch: it was not his responsibility and he had not come for that, but for Jacques Sergent.

"Did he get back home, as expected?"

"As it happens, no. He rang me last night…"

She had of course promised discretion to the man from the third floor, but their conversation had two rather uncontrollable witnesses, Ernest and Frédéric. Therefore impossible to keep it totally concealed.

"What?"

What does he mean, what? Was she supposed to have dragged Fleurus out of bed and trumpeted the news?

"All right, he didn't tell me much. Just that he wasn't coming home right away…"

"When, then?"

"He didn't say."

"Did he say anything else?"

"No."

After this somewhat inexact explanation, Léonie did not think it was worth adding that she had recognized the Chinese woman as one of the characters in the photos, nor that her flowers were highly exotic orchids that one could not get for love nor money in Paris.

Chapter 24

FILIAL LOVE SUITED them better than just Love. Pah became Bouillon's daughter. For registration, she chose a French first name for herself from the list of Saints' names: Nicole. Her adoptive father nevertheless continued to call her Pah. They moved into the pompously named Bellevue district, in the western part of town; an estate of cheap detached houses for junior clerks, each equipped with a little garden. Pah planted some vegetables in theirs. She had quickly learnt some rudimentary French. He tried two or three times to question her about her abduction and her origins. She remained vague. Had she forgotten, or were her memories too painful? Eventually, he wondered whether she feared being sent back home if he ever got to know. He did not persevere.

Together they visited the territory. In particular the islands: Donghai, Naozhou… Bouillon believed these places were uninhabited, or virtually so. Mistake. They accommodated a multitude of walled villages, each bristling with bamboo poles and surmounted by a black stone watchtower. "Against the pirates," said the girl, who presumably knew what she was talking about. The inhabitants cultivated some groundnuts, bred some cattle and, on the coast, they dug strange ponds, filled with a yellowish and stinking substance. "I often cook that for you!" Pah enjoyed saying to Emile with his sensitive stomach. Jelly fish. Pickled or dried, they found their way into a lot of the local dishes.

Sometimes they took a carriage to go to Tche-Kam. In the labyrinth of its dark narrow streets, banners and signs were entangled like a jumble of Mikado sticks. Shop-keepers from another age lived there, buried under their merchandise. Pah bought their spices and other condiments which she could not find anywhere else. The centre of the city boasted a venerable temple with a constant cloud of smoke above its curved roof from the incense, and a blend of scents from the offerings. Bouillon did not go in. He smoked a cigarette in the parvis while his daughter prayed to Buddha, Guanyin, Mazu, the Taoist hermits and thirty-six other divinities of that ilk. They met outside the temple and, just before going back to Fort-Bayard, enjoyed a *tofu fa* dusted with brown sugar.

On Sundays, Emile and Gabriel went to the railway station. Disused and derelict, it no longer looked much like Deauville's, nor Dalat's, nor anywhere's. An old Chinese man had occupied an annex and amassed piles of bric-a-brac. The two railway men did not care. They came for Eliane. They spent the whole day in the depot, polishing and oiling her, checking the state of her brakes or of her boiler while singing songs of the past. They brought their lunch and their wine. At midday they picnicked there. After a little siesta, they continued cleaning their lady. At the end of the day they left her for The Travellers. A shower. Gabriel returned behind his counter, Emile mixed with the first clients who came for aperitif. Happy days. They were even close to thinking that in this remote colony of Fort-Bayard, nothing unpleasant could ever happen again. In order to immortalize these precious moments, Bouillon bought himself a nice camera.

Chapter 25

ROASTED CHICKEN, sautéed potatoes, crème caramel. Plus, for her husband, a nice Burgundy. The dinner concocted by Léonie would not have won a prize for weight loss recipes, but its goal was something quite different: namely to sate Ernest and Frédéric in order to render them in no condition to overhear her telephone conversation with Sergent, especially if she had to note down the combination of his safe and the venue of their rendezvous.

"Where did you get the wine?"

"Don't you like it?"

"Yes, but…" Ernest was sure it must have cost a fortune.

"A present from the Vernets. Don't you remember?"

This couple on the second floor, flat B, from Dijon, had a thriving wine trade and only seldom occupied their Paris flat; two good reasons for them to be credited with an imagined generosity.

"Really good, their plonk! You must say thank you for me."

At two thousand francs for the bottle, and it already half empty, 'really good' it surely had to be.

"Frédéric, you've finished your dessert? So, to your homework now… And tonight, no playing. Off you go! Into your bedroom!"

"But…"

"No buts!"

The child studied much more comfortably at the dining table, as he was in fact used to doing, than in his tiny and gloomy bedroom. He grumbled but obeyed. Normally, Ernest would have promptly condemned his wife for being unreasonable. Heavy with alcohol, he did not say anything. A drunken husband, a son sent into exile… Sergent could now phone without her being excessively anxious. He did so at the agreed time. Léonie picked up the phone, at the same time watching for possible reactions from her family. None apparently: no suspicious half-opening door of her son's bedroom, and nothing but a brief grunt from Ernest, dozing in his armchair.

"Are you still willing to help me? Again, I would understand if…"

"Don't worry."

"Fine. Do you have something to write on? My combination… Its simplicity is rather foolish. It's my date of birth: 09 06 1901."

"Really?"

She was astonished, not so much by the simplicity of the combination but by Sergent's age: fifty-seven. She would have thought five, or even ten, years younger.

"You've written it down?"

"Yes… and… how much?"

"How much what?"

How much what! Despite her surroundings being under control, she did not want to be too explicit.

"Money…"

"Oh, I'm with you. You might as well take it all. God knows when I'll be able to return home.

"OK. The lot… And where…?"

"And where shall we meet?"

"That's right…"

She would have liked to add: *Close by if possible. I can't be too far away from my work, I was already absent because of Antoinette's funeral, etc.* But she didn't.

"Do you know Parc Monceau?"

Chapter 26

O NE DAY WHEN he was going past the Chamber of Commerce, Bouillon noticed an announcement, which had just been posted, for an auction. He went closer to learn more; he would perhaps inform Gabriel, keen reader of such notices. Sometimes boats were sold by auction. Vallée dreamed of a small boat. No, this notice... Rails. A locomotive! The administration was selling them at the end of the month. Inevitable. The railway system was bankrupt, the creditors had to pay themselves from its meagre assets. Inevitable but still sad. In the past, Vallée and he, with great regret, had had to part with locomotives which were too old and had to be scrapped. They were attached to their locos, a bit like to a dog. Eliane? They had run her less than one hundred kilometres but hadn't she too, like them, been betrayed?

"Well, what can we do?" responded Gabriel to whom Emile hastened to announce the news.

"And if..."

The buyer of Eliane would surely be a serious person who would run her on one of the lines which, the Indochinese newspapers reported, would be opened in China, Burma or Siam! He would surely be grateful for their maintaining the locomotive! He would surely need a mechanic and a driver!

"You must be dreaming."

Gabriel was right. Would they give up their new life to go back to the railway? On the eve of the event, Bouillon nevertheless asked Leblanc for the morning off, and persuaded Gabriel to accompany him.

"What? You would like us to buy it? Well, if that would make you happy…"

The sale was taking place in the waiting room of the railway station. Settled right at the back behind a thinly scattered audience, Pioux, the fatalist, nodded gently to himself.

The auctioneer, a tall lanky man who had come from Hanoi, began the session in a lighthearted manner, already convinced that he would not perform miracles but he would at least entertain the gallery. The rails were to be sold in several lots:

"Rare parts, unique even, which yesterday led nowhere… could lead to an excellent deal if you buy them today!"

Soon it was obvious that there were only two bidders: a metals trader from Hong Kong and a rich merchant from Tche-Kam. The trader carried off the first two lots for less than the scrap value of the metal, because retrieval had to be paid by the purchaser. Then it came to the last section of rails, the one that ran through the jungle to the border.

"In all, twenty five kilometres. Reserve price, fifteen thousand piastres!"

Nobody bid.

"Gentlemen, a little effort! Fourteen thousand?"

Even at twelve thousand, no one raised their hand. The auctioneer did not persevere.

"So you don't want rails anymore, fine. You're right to save yourself for the locomotive: a Hohenzollern from the beginning of the century, German made, I can't remember how much horse power because I've lost the sheet of paper, but… a machine that'll last forever. Its reserve price, that I haven't forgotten, thirty thousand piastres!"

The Hong Kong trader guffawed, the merchant spit on

the floor. The rest of the room remained apathetic. Eliane did not find a buyer.

"None of them was worthy of her," Bouillon judged with pride.

The following Sunday, Vallée pretended he had to attend a communion feast at The Travellers in order to avoid going to the depot. The Sunday after that, he felt 'unwell'. Emile understood: his friend was giving up. He carried on the maintenance of Eliane alone.

Chapter 27

*Y*OU MIGHT AS WELL *take it all. God knows when I'll be able to come home.* How long would Sergent be absent for, two, three months? Even five or six... With one or one and a half million, the maximum amount she imagined she would find in his safe, he wouldn't have to worry. If it had been hers, it would have represented a hell of a lot of money and its safe delivery was already causing her a few worries.

She made piles of the Bonapartes (ten thousand franc notes), the Henri IVs (five thousands), the various Richelieus (one thousands) and the Victor Hugos (five hundreds). She added them all up and, not believing it, counted them again. Once... twice. No, there was no mistake: nine million, three hundred and twenty-two thousand francs. There were nine million, three hundred and twenty-two thousand francs in Jacques Sergent's safe! And he wanted her to bring him the whole lot, this afternoon to Parc Monceau where she had never set foot before! She could not even contact him. She would have at least asked that she could make two trips: Don't you understand, my handbag isn't big enough! Or did he even need so much? Who knows with the rich? Sometimes their notion of money is quite different.

It's your fault after all. You should never have accepted so easily, she rebuked herself. Now, it was too late. She had no desire for lunch, and no inspiration for dinner. She did not go shopping. The heavy presence of nine million, three hundred and twenty two thousand francs on the third floor, the security of which the owner had in a way made her responsible for, worried her sick and prevented her from going out. The building had never been burgled before, but didn't the worst misfortunes happen at the worst moments?

Two o'clock. Her rendezvous was at three. She went back to Sergent's flat, trembling. At least the money was still there. She wrapped it up in an old *France Soir* newspaper, and shoved the whole lot into her string bag which, after some thought, she had found to be the most practical and least noticeable to convey the funds in. She closed the safe and carefully, with a cloth, wiped what she had touched then tiptoed out and down the stairs.

"Ah! Madame Burot! I was looking for you!"

Damn! She cursed under her breath while hiding her bulky bag as much as she could rather like an udder between her legs. At the bottom of the stairs, in the hall way, the Baroness de La Brosse was brandishing *L'Intran-sigeant.*

"These journalists, eh? I tell you. Let me congratulate you on giving this young man a good beating! Look how he is treating you now…"

The baroness opened the newspaper and read aloud.

"'Incident on the Rue François Ponsart. Main Witness out of Control!'" increasing her outrage with each word. "A wonderful appetizer, and what follows is not without flavour either:

As promised in my previous article, I had no intention of remaining inactive in solving the enigma of the murder of Antoinette Leroux who was poisoned by a mysterious letter from Hong Kong. So I attended the victim's funeral yesterday. It was a simple, moving and dignified ceremony. What followed was less so. Wishing to stay behind, on my own, after the funeral, and meditate – like

124

Chateaubriand in search of his family members who were victims of the Terror – on the fragility of human life and reflect on who could have perpetrated such a horrible crime, I came face to face with two women. The first, Chinese, around thirty-five years old, was spending a moment of silence at Antoinette Leroux's grave. The second was none other than Léonie Burot, the colleague of the deceased, who had, let me remind you, discovered the body. I had come across her at the funeral. She and I were carefully watching the Chinese woman whom I was attempting – as much to modestly contribute to the official inquiry as to keep you informed, dear faithful readers – to photograph. Suddenly Madame Burot attacked me with all the fury of a harpy while, at the same time, warning the stranger. I cannot even describe the ferocity of this assault which has resulted in my incapacity to work for several weeks, a price one has to pay in my profession, the obligations of which I will not go into here. My concern is for the police, for whom a portrait of the foreigner would have helped move the case forward, and my fear is for Léonie Burot. 'Forgive them for they know not what they do.' This noble quote from the Gospels applies perfectly on her case. Let us not believe that she is in connivance with the murderers but that certain minds reveal themselves to be less strong than others, so modern psychology teaches us. Police interrogations have weakened, to breaking point, the mind of this woman who has such a tough life; raising almost on her own – her husband, a printer, works long hours – a child 'who is not without difficulties at school,' his teachers confided to us. Consequently, what else is there to recommend to Madame Burot but to take a back seat, and to the police, to treat her gently until the inquiry is concluded?"

Léonie, livid, tightened her grip on her string bag like a shipwreck victim on a lifebuoy.

"I am as outraged as you!" said the Baroness still showing indignation. "You mustn't let this go. Write to the director of *L'Intransigeant*, demand that they print a correction!"

"Yes, you're right…"

Forgive them for they know not what they do. It would have been unsafe to say that Léonie could apply this credo when it came to Frank Belval. The correction she was thinking about was not simply of an epistolary nature. A broken arm, a cranial trauma? The junior reporter had been lucky. Had she not been so preoccupied with Sergent's fortune, she would have worked out, on the spot, his hanging, drawing and quartering, and the tearing to shreds of his intimate parts with red hot tongs.

Chapter 28

O NE SUNDAY, Emile found the depot empty. "For God's sake!?" He dashed to the old Chinese man who was sleeping amongst his paraphernalia.

"Where's my loco?" he shouted.

The man kept a frightened silence. Bouillon went outside again, approached a passerby who avoided him as if he were a madman. He rushed to The Travellers. Ambroggiani was sipping a brandy.

"Your machine? It was me…"

A horse-drawn carriage, driven by his men, had come at dawn to tow her to the jungle of Surprise. By order of the Administrator General, who wanted to get rid of her quickly so that the metals trader from Hong Kong could take his rails, an operation planned for the following week.

"But… why?"

"This creature got in everybody's way, right in the centre of town! She's been buried, in other words. Believe me we bloody struggled. She weighs a ton, the bitch!"

For what was Eliane being blamed? Was she contagious with scabies, plague, cholera? And even if she were! Emile turned to Gabriel who was scrubbing his bar utensils and was not saying anything. How could he not protest…?

"What can we do?"

"You knew, you bastard! That's why you didn't come anymore!"

"Stop talking nonsense…"

Emile slammed the door. Eau de Cologne had given the order to exile Eliane? He decided to go and see him. On his front door step, the Administrator General was saying goodbye to some Mandarins from Guang-Zhou-Wan. To each of them, he was reciting some polite words which an interpreter with a large fixed smile was translating. All of a sudden, confusion! The hand that he was shaking would not let go.

"Ha! Monsieur Bouillon, it's a pleasure. To what do we owe the honour…?"

"The honour, my arse!"

The row was brief. Many firm hands grabbed Emile, threw him down the steps and ejected him.

Panting heavily, his face swelling up, he wandered down to the sea. Passing a street vendor, he bought a bottle of rice wine and got drunk, on his own, looking at the ocean.

The next morning, Leblanc in person dragged him out of bed, a rush of words pouring from his mouth: dishonour, folly, irresponsibility, excuses, resignation!

"If you want," Emile groaned weakly.

His chief's anger aggravated his migraine. Pah brought some coffee. Leblanc calmed down.

"All right, we'll try and fix things…"

"Not necessary. You said it, resignation."

"Nonsense! It's not the end of the world. All the same, your promotion, now…"

"I don't care."

Vallée arrived.

"You like it that much, this loco?"

Bouillon did not reply. He himself no longer understood the nature of the links that attached him to the machine. So, explaining this, even to his best pal…

Chapter 29

TALL TREES WITH leaves still green were outlined against the blue sky and formed a picture postcard image. A certain coolness of the air however indicated that autumn was gradually taking possession of Paris.

"Porte Saint-Jean?"

"Straight in front of you," an ice-cream seller told her.

Sergent had suggested that she wait for him near this stone arch, inside Parc Monceau. He probably knew they wouldn't be disturbed there: only one young mother with a pram and two pairs of old men playing cards occupied the benches around. She sat down slightly to one side of them, almost surrounded by a huge clump of rhododendrons. Even if nobody seemed to pay attention to her, she felt embarrassed, aware of being a possible object of gossip, of suspicion even. Something was wrong about her. She had, as she was coming out of her lodge, changed her old grey cardigan for a patterned jacket, bought the year before in Prisunic. Antoinette thought it was very new wave. Flattering, but did the new wave burden themselves with an old patched up string bag when walking around fashionable districts?

Sergent arrived and Léonie forgot her sartorial torments. With his stooping gait, looking drawn, she felt sorry for him. No doubt he had not slept much these last few days. He greeted her seeming sincerely happy to see her again. She would have quite liked to express her compassion to him, if it had not been for her haste to dispose of her consignment.

"It's in my bag," she informed him without further a do.

And in a lower voice:

"I did what you told me: I took everything, nine million, three hundred and twenty-two thousand francs."

"So much?"

"Yes… What do we do now?"

"Can you leave me your bag?"

It was the simplest solution even though the object would seem more incongruous when entrusted to the man of the third floor, flat C, in his elegant striped suit.

"There is a small hole at the bottom. Make sure that it doesn't get any bigger," in exactly the same way she would have advised Frédéric to take care of a new toy. They made sure that nobody was observing them and the string bag changed hands. Léonie instantly felt liberated.

"Let's walk," suggested Sergent.

They reached the lake in the middle of the park whose water vibrated with a soft and golden light.

"This lake is called Naumachie," he indicated.

Having little interest in toponymy, Léonie was dying to talk to him about something else:

"Did you read the articles in *L'Intransigeant*?"

First of all, remove the slur; Belval's words had questioned her reason and her respectability.

"… A pack of lies. Except for the Chinaman. That's true, my son met him in the lobby of our building and what's more, he recognized him in the pictures that were sent to you. Moreover, I haven't told anyone yet, the Chinese woman in the cemetery, well, she appears in the snaps too!"

Sergent remained silent at first, as if he was evaluating the import of this information, then:

"As for your pugilism with the journalist, I don't know what motivated you, but you did the right thing…"

If, as well as the foolish Baroness de La Brosse, the

person who could have been most angry with her approved of her attitude, it meant that she was not totally insane.

"Because, even if he had been able to photograph and identify this woman, all I would have got would have been a surplus of trouble…"

Who would profit if the frivolous Belval put a name to the Chinese woman and shouted it from the roof tops? Realizing that she had been discovered, wouldn't she become more dangerous? Deep inside, Léonie agreed and even more, her similar line of thought to Jacques Sergent, encouraged her to ask:

"You lived there, in Fort-Bayard, didn't you"?

"So the press says!" he avoided the question with a twinkle in his eye.

Chapter 30

IT USUALLY TOOK Bouillon a good four hours at a fast walking pace to get to Eliane. He was not put off by the effort involved, on the contrary. Who else would do it? Apart from one or two hunters, he had never come across anyone on the path. He felt like an old hand at this now. The evening before, ritually, he had prepared his tools. He got up at dawn, to avoid the heat. Pah served him his breakfast, pulling a reproachful face. He had tried, without success, to reason with her: no pirate was hiding in the jungle, where there was nothing to pillage nor to ransom, and the last tigers had been exterminated ages ago.

"How do you know?"

"I've never seen any!"

His daughter refrained from directly mentioning the engine, but didn't she secretly associate it with a demon?

When he set off, the deserted town was wreathing itself in the traces of day. He passed, indifferent, the old railway station, now an indoor market. He reached the ice factory, and beyond, the rice fields which, as one slowly advanced into the season, changed from tender green to old gold. The raised embankment from the old railway line was still there. He took it, as far as a small chapel which marked the beginning of the Jungle of Surprise. There he stopped for a bite to eat: an apple, or a banana, some cold coffee. In front of him, the rails – the lot not sold in the auction and now overgrown with weeds, rusted and loosened from their clamps like the teeth of someone suffering from scurvy – ran deep into the jungle. Monkeys and birds greeted his entry under the foliage with a torrent of cries, and a blanket of humidity fell on him, sticky and sweet-smelling. It hindered his breathing, made his arms and legs heavy; and within five minutes, he was drenched with sweat. Sometimes it rained and the path became a stream of muddy water. But he never gave up, a true knight. After six or seven kilometres, he arrived at the glade into which Ambroggiani had relegated Eliane. Had this brute actually been capable of a little sensitivity in choosing such a place? This bright clearing with corbelled tree ferns always seemed a little magical to him, like an old painting. First he walked around his Eliane, from whom fled hordes of small animals which had found refuge there during the week. This preliminary inspection accomplished, he climbed on board and went through his checklist: braking system, water tank, fire box, smokestack, steam and sand domes, etc. An endless battle. Atrocious climate, bad weather, all sorts of parasites, exuberant vegetation rooted into the slightest hole, oxidation which created blisters on the steel of the main boiler... Eliane had no respite. Bouillon cleaned, scraped, oiled, polished, and started all over again, indefatigably, Sunday after Sunday.

Going home in the evening, he always stopped at The Travellers. Gabriel and he never talked about trains, stations, the Little Belt Railway nor about the events which had brought them to Fort-Bayard. With all the more reason Eliane was even less a topic of conversation. It was as if they had a tacit agreement, as if their friendship, with its new foundations, demanded putting aside this entire episode of their history.

One time, however:

"How is the engine doing?" It was Henriette who teased him.

Had Emile drunk a little more than usual? He replied, euphorically:

"She's never been better!"

Standard response, but Vallée's wife got excited:

"You hear this, Gabriel? Your loco is in great shape… To Eliane!"

Gabriel was not last to raise his glass and Henriette rubbed it in by pouring Emile a second Muscadet:

"You must show her to us one day."

The excursion was decided for the following Sunday. Wawa invited himself and even Pah was willing to go.

She did not see much of the Vallées for, as with Eliane, she feared their bad influence on her father. Knowing that they were behind the idea of the visit, she preferred to keep an eye on them. Bouillon prepared himself as thoroughly as any guide would, making a list of all the things his friends might need. He forgot neither walking canes for their assistance, nor compass and machetes for their reassurance.

Great was his disillusion, in the evening, after the walk.

"It's true it's a long way," Gabriel said, still short of breath.

"I wouldn't like to go there every day," confirmed Henriette.

Just as well! Emile promised himself never to repeat this kind of group tour during which they lunched and took banal photos of themselves in front of Eliane, as if she were nothing more than a common tourist attraction like an ancient monument, a carrousel or a panorama.

Chapter 31

WHEN THEY PARTED, Sergent pulled a few notes from the bag to offer Léonie.

"It's the least I can do…"

She pushed away his hand and wished him good luck.

"Thank you. I promise I won't bother you again."

She would have gladly told him not to be silly.

The Metro, the stairs, the turnstile, the ticket-puncher, the platform, the bitter cold current of air announcing the arrival of the train, the screeching of the brakes, the ebbing and flowing of the passengers getting off and on, the train moving out again, entering the tunnel, *du bo, du bon, Dubonnet*… So, she was going home as if nothing had happened, when she had just delivered nine million francs to a man whom others wanted to kill, part of a murky drama which had begun twenty years ago in China. The thing was that, in the end, Antoinette was right: Sergent may not be a spy but he certainly had a double life. Sitting opposite her, a middle aged man, unshaven, was drifting off. A jolt from time to time sent the back of his head banging against the seat. The thread of his dreams being broken, he winced briefly then gradually resumed his position… until the next jolt. Did he, like Sergent, also have a double life, this stranger who seemed to be already struggling with his single one? Improbable but, at the same time: didn't the best stories on the subject owe their success to their unlikelihood? For all that, Sergent had partially revealed his alter ego: They are hunting for me… And in the park, hadn't she sensed a quiver in his voice, distress in his eyes? Was it fear? Yes, without a doubt, although not ordinary fear, not intense yet short-lived, not like a scare in the dark or the fright of those who see a ghost. This was rather, something oozing, insidious, like a fever caused by an incurable, tropical disease which stays with you for the rest of your life.

Wagram station. The unshaven one got off. Never go by appearances, but Léonie doubted that he was returning home to a princess in a palace or that he was about to rob a bank. An old man in an overcoat, and with the physique of a clearly non-double life, replaced him. And how many lives did Sergent's enemies have? What did they do apart from hunting him? Even more than for their prey, Léonie conjectured some pathology in them. Would ordinary murderers have sent photographs of themselves to their target? At least they retained a touch of humanity. Why had the Chinese woman ventured to Saint-Ouen to put flowers on Antoinette's grave, the accidental victim, so to speak, of their disastrous enterprise, if not to beg her forgiveness? Her forgiveness… suddenly Léonie was seized with a terrible fear of her own. She too had contributed to the killing of her friend! *I am a criminal!* she felt like bellowing in the old man's ear. No, of course not; nobody gives themselves away like this. Although, Sergent had clearly let her perceive his distress, and the Chinese woman had repented in a spectacular and risky manner. So, why not her? Why wasn't she able to do as they had done? For a split second, perhaps, she envied them. La Muette, her stop. She got off just in time. The doors snapped closed behind her back.

An avant-garde neon in the shape of a lily was shining like a UFO hovering above the shop Passy-Flore, opposite the exit of the underground. Léonie never bought flowers therefore she only knew the florist because she had seen her in other shops in the neighbourhood. The thought of entering her shop embarrassed her for only a split second. A bell jingled and Madame Germaine – which is how the butcher greeted her – emerged from her roses, tulips and gladioli like a carnival queen bearing a somewhat unstable candy floss hairdo.

"Madame Burot, what a surprise! How's the investigation?"

"I have no idea. The police haven't come to see me for a long time."

The last visit by Fleurus was only the day before, but it felt like an eternity to her.

"You want to buy some flowers?"

"Well… er… Do you sell orchids?"

With a wry face Madame Germaine sized up her visitor. Orchids? No, she didn't sell orchids. Her clientele, as posh as they were, didn't ask for them. And that a caretaker should be interested in them… Unless she was mistaken: were they really talking about the same thing? Léonie endeavoured to remain courteous:

"It's only out of curiosity. I was wondering… do people grow them in France, or do they have to be brought from another country?"

The florist knitted her brows again. And then, suddenly:

"I remember now, once, a long time ago, someone asked for orchids! A secretary from I forget which embassy, Thailand or Tahiti, for a reception."

"Aha? And you found some?"

"I didn't, but Blanche did."

"Who is Blanche?"

"A colleague. We started work together in the Boulevard Saint-Germain, at La Rose de France. We stayed there two

139

or three years. Then we went our separate ways, as one says. Blanche got fixed up in the greenhouses in Auteuil. She's still there. I sent the embassy woman to her, because they grow orchids over there."

"The greenhouses in Auteuil?"

"Yes. Go and see her and tell her I sent you."

Within ten minutes, Léonie had done her shopping for dinner – she deserved a bit of a treat, didn't she? Ready-grilled pig's trotters and celery remoulade: a dish which Ernest and Frédéric appreciated only marginally but which she loved. After all, she had handed the money to Jacques Sergent and might soon find out where the Chinese woman's flowers had come from.

Chapter 32

THE SUMMER OF 1939 was so hot and so dry that Eau de Cologne decided to ration water. The colony was annoyed with the Administrator General and, since the latter would not change his decision, with just about anything and everything else too; decidedly neurasthenic. After a few weeks, everyone having more or less got things off their chest, the territory huddled up into a resigned torpor. Life became a long wait. Didn't the end of August, every year, bring about revitalising storms?

"We are living a vegetative life like a cactus which blooms only after a heavy rain," expounded Amyot one evening at The Travellers, in front of a sparse audience.

The attendance at Gabriel and Henriette's café had gone down as much as the water in the Ma-Tse River. The heatwave should have drawn thirsty people to their counter; on the contrary, it made them hide at home. The fault was the ice factory's which had been out of order right from the start of the hot days and unable to be repaired for a long while. The supplier in Hanoi, where the spare parts had to be shipped from, had run out of stock because all the fridge retailers in Tonkin had experienced the same problem at the same time. No more ice cubes for the pastis, not worth going for aperitif!

30th August. Still waiting for rain and spare parts.

31st, same story.

1st September:

"Last year it started to thunder on 27th August," assured Henriette in order to underline the unpredictability of the pluvial season.

"Speaking of thunder," said a worried Amyot using the parallel, "did you hear that it's turning really nasty in Europe? Hitler has just invaded Poland."

"I said 27th, but on second thoughts I wonder if it was not on the 26th…"

"Maybe you're right. Poland is going to resist…"

The deluge that came down during the night washed out the placards that Eau de Cologne had just had plastered all over Fort-Bayard. In the morning, the red and black streaks which stained the Calls for Mobilization looked like an excess of blood and thunder. They lacked credibility. Every year Hitler acquired another piece of Europe but, seen from Fort-Bayard, the menace seemed less real. Most people were hoping, without admitting it, that it would stay that way, but at the same time, wasn't this hope tainted with cowardice? Children of Fort-Bayard, what is your contribution to the struggle against the enemy? Was it their fault if they lived ten thousand kilometres away from their endangered homeland?

Eau de Cologne summoned his countrymen.

"Everyone must join his unit as soon as possible!"

Protestations… Quiet at first, but then more open. Amyot found the affair totally absurd. He had done his military service in Compiègne, in the Corps of Engineers. Was he really going to be forced to go back there?

"What does the word mobilization mean if not just that?" replied the chief of the territory who detailed the logistics of the operation before closing the meeting.

The audience lingered; weren't there supposed to be drinks despite the circumstances? Bouillon and Vallée left. Under the porch of the building, they saw Leblanc, leaning against a column.

"I hadn't counted you among the grumblers," he fired at them, yet with a gentle sarcasm in his voice, quite unusual for him.

"If we have to go, well, we'll go," Gabriel sighed.

"Wise decision. I was actually declared unfit for service. So, I'm staying, obviously."

He did not seem to be delighted about it.

In the end, Fort-Bayard counted only a handful of mobilized, most of whom were left stranded in the ports of Indochina and simply returned to their posts after the defeat of France. The conflict however was not without bringing a few changes. Eau de Cologne disappeared to follow people who identified themselves with a certain free France and a certain General de Gaulle. A nickname for his successor, abrupt and pretentious, quickly came into common use: Abusive Curt. But the big surprise was the Japanese. Of course they were already lurking in the area before the war. The neighbouring islets of Pratas and Lintin and then Hainan Island, a much larger prey, had fallen into their hands. One nevertheless thought that they only had their eyes on China. The French capitulation had whetted their appetite. Vichy and Tokyo had concluded the Agreement for the Joint Defense of Indochina. Nobody was fooled by this diplomatic appellation: the Japanese had the colony at its mercy but, magnanimously let the French retain *sovereignty*. The latter, in return, *granted* their army some facilities. In other words, the Japanese did not invade, but were invited in by their *hosts*. Their Zero fighter planes were taking off from Tourane, their infantry was camped near Saigon. And completely in accordance with the role of an altruistic protector, they had even felt obliged to open a military mission in Guang-

Zhou-Wan with a chief, Colonel Ito, three or four other officers and a platoon of about twenty soldiers. Their presence did not annoy anybody; on the contrary, many praised the efficiency of their early days. Convinced that the Chinese were smuggling out at sea in the channels between Donghai and Naozhou, where French law and order never prevailed more than sporadically, one of their launches had patrolled the zone for two or three weeks. It hadn't been much fun: a dozen junks were sent to the bottom. Not only had the Land of the Rising Sun been successful where France had failed but moreover, the wrecks turned out to be wonderful lobster pots. Gabriel, who had in the end bought himself a rowing boat, often went to them with Wawa. "It's starting to be known," they were sorry to say. Soon they would stop going. Unless… "The Japs sink more boats." Unlikely. Abusive Curt had given in and banned all transit of Chinese goods via Fort-Bayard. Calmed, the Japanese military mission had eased up. *Beach in the morning, brothel in the evening. Like everyone else here!* People laughed at this sally, without really knowing why. No one in Gwang-Zhou-Wan really lived like that, yet the whole territory revelled in this caricature of themselves.

Hostilities raged all around and refugees converged on the border. They told horror stories that were only half believed. A few were allowed to enter, but was it the right thing to do? In this war, one ended up not understanding anything anymore. Who were your friends, who were your enemies? For example Chiang Kai-Shek, head of the Nationalist Government in Chongqing: Vichy and he were still officially on good terms, but for how long? The troops of the Generalissimo had recently removed one hundred and eighty kilometres of rails of the Yunnan railway, built and run by France. All this so that the Japanese could not use them... Not a good way to behave. These rails, which they had then put back together elsewhere, were not really theirs. And the Americans? Not well behaved either. For a while not only did they arm the Chinese, but they also bombarded the Japanese positions. They were probably going to end up launching a few projectiles on Hanoi, Saigon... and Guang-Zhou-Wan. Would the Japanese protect Fort-Bayard?

"Never in a million years! The French defend the French," maintained Vallée; for a company of the 19th Regiment of Mixed Colonial Infantry had also occupied their quarters and were charged with pushing back any foreign aggressor. They would defend to the last man if there was trouble, the Japanese wouldn't. The captain of the 19th was Lefébure, a Parisian. He and his men, when they were off duty, turned up at The Travellers for a drink. *Nice lads.*

Chapter 33

LÉONIE GOT OFF the train at the same time as a crowd of men in flat caps, bearing binoculars and newspapers. She would not have been surprised to see Fleurus' colleague, Verger, among them. The racegoers headed towards the track and she towards the greenhouses.

"Blanche has lunch at work. Between twelve and two, you can be sure to find her. A small red-haired plump woman, you can't miss her." Perfectly matching the picture drawn by Madame Germaine, an employee wearing a green overall and sitting on a wicker chair in the middle of a rock garden was biting into a fresh tomato.

"Hello. You're not Blanche by any chance, are you?"

"Yes, that's me…"

"I've been sent by Germaine, in the Passy Flore flower shop…"

"Ah! How is she?"

"Fine," Léonie answered reflexively.

She could tell her later that she did not know the florist very well.

"I had tomatoes for lunch too," she added.

Inventing a simple common denominator with a stranger would always smooth the path for a conversation.

"Not this type surely! Saint-Vincent tomatoes. They come directly from my home town, in the Loiret."

"No! Really? You too are from the Loiret?"

"From Lorris."

"I'm from Boynes!"

From there it was easy going: no need to complicate things anymore and invent half-true stories to justify her sudden interest in orchids. Blanche did not care. Giving some information to someone from back home was part of regional solidarity.

"Orchids? You've come to the right address. The tropical green house is just next door. Follow me…"

"Oh!"

The heavy humid atmosphere surprised the caretaker, and the strong perfumes made her feel dizzy.

"What are they like, your orchids?"

"Small, purplish…"

"The leaves, wide or slender?"

"The thing is…"

Léonie marvelled at the shimmer and the texture of the flowers.

"American, African or Asian?"

The question puzzled her for a moment. But wasn't the answer obvious?

"Asian. Like these, only a little darker…"

"*Aerides. Aerides roseum* or *Aerides rubescens*. They come from Asia. It's written here…"

Blanche handed Léonie a small slip taken from a pot:

"Sikkim, Thailand, Vietnam, Laos, South China."

"These orchids, how do you get hold of them?"

"The Aerides? We grow them ourselves. It's not difficult, we always have seedlings. If you want, I can give you some…"

"Thank you, but no. And the rarer varieties?"

"If they haven't yet been acclimated to France, of course we must import them."

"Is it… easy?"

"You must be joking! We need a license. Plus there is the quarantine. Only specialized nurseries like us can do that."

She could be getting somewhere…

"Apart from you, these specialized nurseries, are there many of them?"

"For orchids? No!"

"How about in Paris?"

"In Paris, you've got Jardin des plantes and two or three private companies: André and Lebel in Montmorency, Carlino and Sons in Jouy, Comptoir Floral Jean Pioux in Rambouillet. I don't know any others…"

"And do you know the people who work there?"

"A little bit, of necessity."

"There wouldn't be a Chinese lady, would there?"

"At Pioux's, yes. Miss Bah or Pah. But how would you know…?"

Far too complicated to explain! Léonie simply contented herself with warmly embracing her new and invaluable friend.

Chapter 34

WHEN PIOUX, looking nervous and shifty, appeared suddenly at The Travellers, one late afternoon, Gabriel thought he hadn't seen him since the beginning of the war, although he wouldn't stake his life on it. In actual fact, the man mixed less and less with the local society. He did not like the people in Fort-Bayard and vice versa.

The scandal of the railway, still vivid in people's memory, played a large part in this. They reproached Pioux for his inability to see what was going on. How could he, as co-director of the operating company, have been so easily duped by Claret-Llobet, taking all the people of Guang-Zhou-Wan with him in his fall? For the story damaged even a little more the already dubious reputation of the colony, and led to additional jibes from the expatriates: "What were you promised this year? A casino? The World Expo?"

Pioux's fierce and spectacular comeback was not much appreciated either. It seemed somewhat shady. Although ruined, he had in less than four years paid back all his debts and started – which is how people learned that in his youth he had studied agronomy – a horticulture business. His specialty? Rare flowers which he brought back from remote forests in Yunnan or Upper Tonkin, where he dealt with the strange people who lived there. His enterprise was going so well that he had opened a branch in Hanoi, to supply the Indochinese elite.

"What can I get you?"

Pioux hesitated, as if he had not come to drink.

"A lemonade," he ordered in the end.

"We don't see you very often these days?" Vallée filled the silence.

"I'm very busy. I spent the first half of the month in Hanoi. By the way, I met the Oliveira brothers… They've asked me to inform you that they are cancelling their visit next month, and therefore their reservation. 'The war doesn't encourage people to buy clothes', they told me. Apparently last time, they just made enough to cover their travelling expenses."

"Thank you for informing us. Another one?"

Although the news was not good, the messenger's effort was worth rewarding.

"Why not? Listen, I also want to tell you about something else…"

"Oh yes?" said Vallée, affecting surprise. He thought it strange that Pioux, with that agitated mood of his, had only come to pass on the message from the Portuguese.

"It also concerns Bouillon. When is he next coming here?"

"Probably tonight."

They met at The Travellers, at closing time, Pioux on one side of the bar, Gabriel and Emile on the other.

"I have some information about Claret-Llobet," he confided, conspiratorially.

The Oliveira brothers had affirmed:

"… He is hiding in Macau!"

Hiding, in fact, was not the appropriate term. The swine was living there openly, under a new name: Major Buffet, on leave from the Republican Guard. But the twins had positively identified him.

"Believe it or not, he and the General Tax Farmer, Dos Santos, have become inseparable."

"Dos Santos?" repeated Bouillon, shocked.

"Himself. It leaves you speechless, doesn't it?"

Dos Santos! The incident of the *Wing On*! Leblanc's favourite tale about the setbacks of the opium market.

"The *Wing On*, yes Monsieur Bouillon," continued Pioux reading his mind. "Well, I think a second episode is being set up…"

Casimir's ex-associate tapped on the bar, like a card player after an opening he thinks will unsettle everyone around the table.

"The Officers' Club, have you heard of it? It's the smartest club in Macau. Dos Santos and the pseudo Major Buffet dined there only ten days ago. Not alone. Another fellow joined them…"

Pioux resumed his tapping, waiting for them to ask who.

"Seng Loon-Fat! The Lobster!"

"Dear God!"

Deprived of his license and kicked out of Fort-Bayard, Seng had not remained unemployed long. The Kuomintang had just created a *Bureau for the Prohibition of Opium* in Canton which in actual fact was a monopoly for its production and trade.

The Lobster, very much in favour with the nationalists, was managing it. Under his leadership, Canton and its environs were covered with opium poppies up to the Mount of the Seven Goats, the legendary origin of the town. The fall of the city to the Japanese had only forced him to move his plantations to Chongqing, following in the wake of the Chiang Kai-Shek government.

"You can imagine the kind of discussions that this bunch of crooks would have had… Seng, in Chongqing, is obviously looking for juicy incomes from his merchandise. What better clients than Dos Santos in Macau, and

Casimir who didn't lack the ability to handle Indochinese gangsters: the Corsicans of Saigon for example?"

Emile and Gabriel wondered about the whole thing. Was this scenario plausible? Japan controlled most of the territories between Chongqing and Macau. Could the opium of the Lobster possibly get through their nets? As for Casimir, wasn't Pioux exaggerating when he pretended that he was in the good books of the Corsican mafia in Saigon?

"I'll inform Leblanc," promised Bouillon nevertheless.

The affair, if proved to be true, would constitute a huge humiliation to Customs and Excise.

"What do you want him to do?"

"I don't know... raise a protest."

"I admit that I couldn't care less about Leblanc's protests..."

"How about if somebody brought an action against Claret-Llobet in Macau?" intervened Gabriel.

There was still a warrant against him, for fraud, embezzlement and other crimes. Didn't police forces cooperate with each other?

"No. I checked. There is no extradition agreement between Portugal and France, neither between Macau and Indochina."

"Of course not!" brayed Vallée.

"Never mind: I have a better plan."

A pause and Pioux delivered coldly: "We capture Claret-Llobet ourselves and we bring him back here to be tried."

154

Chapter 35

RAMBOUILLET? But that's miles away! And such a lot of effort to discover what? An unscrupulous gang who would probably kidnap her... and who would look after the lodge while she was away? She had often been absent these last few days. For Antoinette's funeral it was legitimate, but Parc Monceau and the greenhouses in Auteuil...? And if there were a water leak at the baroness's, whose ten year warranty on her water pipes had long since expired, or if Madame Couquiaud had a heart attack, it would be catastrophic. She was on the point of giving up, of notifying Fleurus: *Voila. I have located the Chinese woman. It's Mademoiselle Bah, or Pah, and she works in Rambouillet in a horticulture enterprise specialising in exotic flowers. Your responsibility now.* But no. She ended up at Montparnasse station, amid the odours of cider and coal, then in the railcar going to Chartres.

"Rambouillet, a two-minute stop!" Although only fifty kilometers from Paris, the place confused her as much as a remote region.

"Rue Gambetta?"

A passer-by pointed it out to her. The street in question radiated affluence and calm.

Jean Pioux Establishment – Flowering and Ornamental Plant Nursery - Import and cultivation of plants from overseas - China and Asia – was established there, at number 1. A stone wall topped with wrought iron and entangled with wisteria concealed almost the entire interior. Léonie ruled out the idea of pretending to be a client for, at the cemetery, the Chinese woman must have had time to see her face. She gently pushed open the gate and discovered a small gravelled courtyard and two buildings in the shape of an L. The first one, covered with Virginia creeper was a private residence. From the second, a greenhouse, she heard voices. She went towards it and, spotting a window ajar, peeped in. A heavy humidity hit her just like at Blanche's, but what a shambles, light-years away from the very orderly Auteuil! Lopsided shelves sagged under flower pots, seedbeds in tubs, bags of compost and fertilizer; a wooden altar with red and bearded deities was slotted in this mess like a washing machine in a rubbish dump; and finally a machine, a large metallic casing from which sprouted a pipe ending in a giant shower head. At regular intervals and with a noise resembling that of a tire being deflated, the head spat out a tepid mist which blended languidly with the air inside the greenhouse.

Four people were sitting at a work table right underneath an unusually large fan secured on the ceiling of the structure. She immediately identified two of them: her son's Chinaman, without either a cap or 'thick glasses', and Mademoiselle Pah, or Bah. Léonie understood why, on the pictures dating twenty years earlier, the young lady did not smile. Her gold teeth literally shone in her mouth! The third person, a short-legged man in his sixties, wearing a vest, sat with his back to her, offering only the sight of his balding bumpy head. There remained the fourth one, wizened and morose, he was huddled up, deep in a wheel chair and, with a bony and hesitating hand, was picking at a saucer of peanuts. He chewed each mouthful with an extreme slowness, giving the impression that he could never swallow it. Léonie thought about the monkeys in the zoo at Vincennes, dismally despondent in their cages. Even so, she managed to recognize in this human wreck, thanks to his thin moustache which looked to have been drawn on, one of the two European men posing in front of the locomotive, in the photos sent to Sergent.

The greenhouse was distorting the voices, and most of the conversation was incomprehensible to the caretaker. She could make out little more than the names by which the four addressed each other, in raised voices:

"You, Wawa…"

"Me, with Emile and Pah…"

"And you, Jean?"

'Jean' – for Jean Pioux without doubt – the man showing his back and wearing a vest, suddenly raised his voice.

"This bastard… enough to calm him down!"

He pronounced these last words opening a drawer from which he took a black and shiny object he passed around. A pistol! Léonie, scared, hastily stepped back and banged her head against the corner of the open window.

"Ouch!"

When she recovered, the gun had got back into Pioux's hands and the crossed eyes on his Eurasian face shone like blowlamps.

Her frantic sprint all the way to the station reminded her of the nightmares where she ran like a mad woman toward an endlessly receding goal. She did not look back, but for a long time felt the fiery eyes of the horticulturist on her back.

"What time is the next train?" out of breath, she asked at the counter.

"Where to?"

"Anywhere! The next train out!"

Brest or Quimper, she would have taken either.

The railway timetables decided for her:

"Paris. In five minutes."

On the platform, she stayed close to the stationmaster, ready to cry for protection if… Five minutes to wait? In other words an eternity. Fortunately, the criminals of rue Gambetta did not pursue her, and the railcar eventually arrived.

Chapter 36

T HEY DIDN'T SEE anything of Macau. The *Lisboa*, the steamship taking them to the Portuguese colony, although sailing in waters guaranteed safe by the Japanese, hit a mine, the origin of which was unknown. Serious damage fore and three injured, one seriously. The captain turned back. "Fate was against us," deplored Pioux. Vallée went back to The Travellers and Bouillon to Customs and Excise.

"There'll be other opportunities for you to go to Macau," Leblanc said to console Bouillon. "Having said that, it's not so easy to kidnap people."

Emile's face turned red. "You knew?"

"Word of the project had indeed reached my ears. On the day of your departure to be exact. This Buffet, who in fact could be Claret-Llobet… I absolutely understand your motivations, although…"

"It's true, I should have mentioned it to you. Especially as Claret-Llobet seems to be in it with Dos Santos and Seng Loon-Fat…"

Leblanc gestured dismissively, signifying his assistant had not told him anything new.

"A repeat of the *Wing On*? Some friends of mine have also told me this tale which they heard from Pioux himself. A real chatterbox that one, but never mind. I for one maintain there is nothing today that allows us to seriously think that any sort of plot could be hatched between Chongqing, Macau and the rest of the world. Even if Dos Santos, Seng and your Claret-Llobet had indeed met, what would this prove?"

If the reunion of three such utter scoundrels did not affect the director of Customs and Excise more than that, what would it take to make him react?

"... To be honest all this matters little to me. For, let's admit it, if you insist that those three are conspiring together, do you believe they are capable of succeeding? I don't."

How had Leblanc been able to put up with the fact that Dos Santos, Seng and Casimir, right in the middle of a war, had built up a network of refining and distributing opium when he was at the head of a sterile refinery, deprived of raw material because of the conflict? Bouillon went back to his statistics-tax.

Chapter 37

THE GANG FROM Rambouillet would respond; it was inevitable. Why did she so carelessly throw herself into the lion's den? To help Sergent? *Idiot! You still don't know where he is.*

Ding-dong! The lodge's bell rang. She shivered. Already the murderers? Not in broad day light! Salsify then? She peeped through the window.

Oh no, not that creep again! It was Philibert, her *friend* from the cemetery, clad in a drab suit and grasping a briefcase to his midriff which put a final touch to his extremely weird look. Unfortunately, just as she drew the curtain half open, he looked in her direction. He gestured to show that he had seen her. Impossible to ignore him now; she opened the door, grumbling.

"What brings you here? And your friend Dédé isn't with you?" as though she doubted that he could go anywhere without him. But he took the question as an invitation.

"Can I come in for a moment? I have things to show you," he said pointing to his briefcase.

Here we go! The grossest of tricks… She had neither the time nor the desire to see them and even less to go through them: these 'things' he wanted to show her!

"I'm taking time off from work to do this," he insisted.

You should have used it to go to the cinema or the fun fair, she rebuked him in her mind.

"It's about the inquiry."

"Surprise surprise!" Slightly better, but still smelling of pretext.

"Yesterday, I saw your policeman, Fleurus…"

Lies. Or just a coincidence? Once, in the Bois de Boulogne, she had actually bumped into Madame de Lattre, the wife of Marshal de Lattre, as she was coming out of the Pré Catelan restaurant. So…

"Didn't I mention that I work at the Ministry of Foreign Affairs?"

What next! As an ambassador perhaps? And what has this got to do with Salsify?

"… At the records office, to be more precise."

"A good job, I don't doubt…"

"As it happens, the inspector came to check the file on Fort-Bayard."

"Oh!"

Couldn't he have been more explicit earlier, this dull half-wit? Caution, though, the story of the archives could still be a trick.

"… Not more than ten minutes, all right?"

Léonie asked the zealous character to sit in Ernest's armchair, which was difficult to get up from. If he dared to have some salacious intention, she would be ready for him and could see it coming a mile off.

"So, yesterday," started the archivist, "Inspector Fleurus turned up and asked for the file on Fort-Bayard. 'Which years?' I ask him. '37, 38, 39, around those,' he answers. 'In that case, you need a special authorization for documents less than sixty years old,' I explain to him. 'What? But I am from the police!' Then he went and complained to my chief. Gordon Bennett! Police or not, it makes no difference. He'll have to come back with a letter from his superiors. Then we have to clear it all with the Quai d'Orsay. In short, there's a lot to do."

"And so?"

Was it simply to relate Salsify's bad luck that this oaf was making all this fuss? And what has this got to do with her? Irritated, she shot him an angry look. He seemed agitated, opened his mouth to speak, closed it again, glanced shiftily from left to right, fidgeted some more on his seat and at last opened his briefcase from which he pulled out a sheet of paper faded with age: the carbon copy of an old, typed letter.

"You do realise that I'm not allowed to take documents out of the office, but for you… Shall I read it to you?"

"Please yourself."

He cleared his throat.

"Fort Bayard, 12th February 1936,
From: Adm Gen. GZW
To: Gov. Gen. Indochina.
Your Excellency,

It is with some dismay that I am writing to inform you, after a thorough investigation of all the elements, alas incontestably true, of a most painful event which has just happened in Guang-Zhou-Wan: Casimir de Claret-Llobet, the champion of the railway which was supposed to link the capital of our territory with the Chinese border, has, the day after the inauguration of the line, disappeared, stealing the finances of the company, a sum, according to the agent of the Bank of Indochina who was managing the accounts, of almost a million piastres.

Needless to say I will take my share of responsibility. However, I would like to remind you that I have never given my unreserved support to this project, when on the contrary some in Hanoi – you may only have been partially informed about this – chose to back it uncondi-tionally. In their defence, because I do not wish to denigrate anyone in particular, the credulity was wide-

163

spread, even the banks were deceived as well as the
principal associate of Casimir de Claret-Llobet, one Jean
Pioux, despite his undeniable principles and integrity. Be
that as it may, I have without delay alerted all our police
forces in Indochina and those in neighbouring countries to
arrest and lock up the outlaw…

Yours etc., etc.,

Jules Bassot, Administrator General of Guang-Zhou-
Wan."

Philibert fell silent, his eyes eagerly seeking some gratitude from Léonie, who was stunned but not wanting to show it.

"Don't you think that Jacques Sergent could be…?"

Casimir de Claret-Llobet? No, Léonie did not think: it had nothing to do with reasoning, it was blatantly obvious. At the same time, though, she felt an uneasiness coming over her. Strangely enough, the revelation that Sergent was possibly a crook, altering the idyllic image she had had of him until now, did not shock her. Her unease was to do with something else. Fleurus, in a few days, would also find out about the scandal of the Fort-Bayard railway. He was certainly no genius, but he too would probably reach the conclusion that the letter from Hong Kong was addressed to none other than the man whose crime had just been narrated by the archivist. But just why did this bother her so?

In the mean time…

"See you again? The thing is, as you can see, I'm rather busy… Your telephone number? It would be better if I had it…?"

Philibert slipped a piece of paper into her hand and pressed her palm insistently. His hungry eyes were searching, deep into hers, looking for collusion which they did not find. She, indifferent, read disappointment in his.

"See you soon?"

"Oh yes?" she answered before closing her door.

Chapter 38

Y ET ANOTHER 14th of July, and Bouillon had a feeling that all these unproductive years were piling up like clutter in an attic.

This particular National Day he would play truant. He would not join the procession of officials who were going to lay a wreath on the graves of the French soldiers in the cemetery of Haitou; he would not watch the Indigenous Guard's Parade augmented this year by that of a detachment of the 19th Lefébure; he would not stuff his face at Abusive Curt's with nibbles and sparkling wine – which, in these times of austerity, replaced champagne.

Rebellion? Not quite. But a dream, last night, from which he remembered only incoherent but painful snatches: he had found himself in the clearing where Eliane still lay. He was tied to the locomotive, both hands and feet. Why? He didn't know. A horde of faceless beings burst out of the jungle. They encircled him, broke into a macabre dance. He struggled, in vain. The locomotive moved. Her cylindrical body started vibrating, her boiler reddened, her smokestack coughed out an acrid cloud. A herd of buffalo joined in with the dancers. Beings and animals soon formed a single meld. He himself changed. His feet! His joints cracked, his flesh stretched, hair grew on his body and hoofs replaced his toes. The whole meld fell on him. The flash of a sabre, a stab of pain… His hoofs were chopped off and thrown into Eliane's boiler. Then suddenly he was in Paris, La Rapée-Bercy railway station. Gabriel, Léon, Aubin, all his old colleagues of the Little Belt laughing while enjoying a stew prepared with his flesh, and forcing a spoonful down his throat. He screams or, rather, he lows.

Was it the climate, or a kind of debasement of the mind brought about by local conditions? Sometimes he felt that between reality and dream other states crept in. Didn't his dream hold some premonition? He wanted to be sure. This was his own problem. He disregarded Pah's plea to postpone it till Sunday and did not inform anybody, not even Leblanc who told him the day before: "See you tomorrow. Perhaps the celebration won't be that bad."

So, departure at dawn as usual. The indoor market, the ice factory, the paddy fields… It was a nice day, his hike was easy: he felt light on his feet and in his heart, a kind of fulfilment gradually chased away the distressing heaviness of his dream. The chapel, the jungle with its intense odour… This dream, how idiotic and yet how wonderful to have had it! Its only goal was to liberate him. From now on he would evade the frivolities, the constraints. *You must live according to your desire.* He walked the whole distance in only two hours. Upon his arrival, a horde of small multicoloured birds flew out of Eliane's smokestack which he caressed, finding the metal warmed by the sun. It was a pleasant sensation. His locomotive was really magnificent. He climbed on board, cleared the firebox door of invading creepers and opened it…

"Arghh…!" He was petrified, speechless, amazed. The furnace was full, full to bursting, from the bottom to the top, with wooden crates. Furiously he pulled one out. Engraved, on the top, it bore the mark of Customs and Excise of Indochina. He unsealed it with the crowbar which he kept in the cab. Inside, boxes, familiar. He looked inside the boiler again. A quick count. Off hand, about

168

twenty crates: all the opium of the refinery of Fort-Bayard!

"The bastards!" He extracted a box from the opened crate, put it in his bag and ran back. "Oh God!" In his hurry, he had just tripped over a sleeper and fallen between the rails. No damage done, but another revelation. Right under his nose, a small brown object in the grass: the butt of a cigar. The royal blue ring emblazoned with a phoenix was still fitted around it. A Hatamen, so dear to Casimir de Claret-Llobet.

Chapter 39

"ANYTHING NEW?"
"No."
"*Bon appétit*, then!"

The first course, herring and potato salad, was eaten in silence. Since his wife had 'chastised' Franck Belval, Ernest beheld her in a new light. It was one thing to *rebuke an imbecile*, but breaking his arm and half-smashing his skull was quite another; revealing in her an unexpected, even worrisome, temperament.

As for Léonie, she was not going to tire her husband with an account of her incursion into Rambouillet, and risk reprisal. She could do without him moaning at her between noisy mouthfuls of herring.

"Shall I switch on the radio?" suggested Frédéric, unused to silence between his parents.

A vague approval. The set crackled a bit. They caught the end of Michel Debré's speech: "… Long live the Republic! Long live France!" Ham omelette, Fire in an old people's home plunges the town of Laon into mourning: three dead, ten injured, dilapidated buildings, incompetent management. Camembert, Gina Lollobrigida taking a break in Hotel Rafael: *Buongiorno Parigi*! Fruit salad, the weather forecast, Baroness de La Brosse…

Léonie's ally was knocking at the door of the lodge, waiving a roneoed copy.

"Have you seen this? It was slid under my doormat."

The caretaker thought she saw the word 'PETITION'. This was confirmed when the baroness calmed down and she saw the whole text:

171

To monsieur Aimé Duflot, head of the management committee of 11, rue François Ponsart.

I, the undersigned .... owner / tenant (delete where applicable)

of – ... floor, flat – circle A, B, C or D –

having learned of the cowardly attack that Madame Léonie Burot, presently the caretaker of my building, has carried out on monsieur Franck Belval, chief reporter of L'Intransigeant,

a) Declare that her unspeakable, ignominious, violent and dangerous behaviour is incompatible with her duties as a caretaker;

b) Request, consequently, her immediate dismissal.

Date and signature.

"Guess who is orchestrating this campaign..."

"Madame Belval?"

"Who else? She is the personification of vulgarity. Have no fear, I will not sign and I doubt whether other people will support this libel. However, if I were you..."

Léonie did not hear either what the baroness was suggesting she should do if she were her, nor the call for calm from Ernest, who feared that after the nephew, his wife might decide to do even worse to the aunt. Libellers, murderers, everyone was against her. She now perceived the world as only a vast ruin.

A sleepless night. When she was not listening for the slightest noise, she was assessing the chances of Belval's petition succeeding. Who, in the building, would approve of this wicked woman? And what would the management committee do if she won over the majority? In any case, wouldn't the Chinese have murdered her before this happened? At four thirty, not able to stand it any longer, she got up. If she was not going to sleep, she might as well make some headway in doing her work. A hasty wash, a quick coffee in the kitchen. She left the lodge and opened her gate. It was still dark. The street light cast a dim reflection on the marble of the hallway. To the Devil with all these thoughts: on to the dustbins! She manhandled the first onto her trolley and pushed it out onto the pavement.

"Madame Burot?"

Léonie heard her heartbeat as clearly as with a stethoscope. On the other side of the street, no more than five meters from her, Mademoiselle Pah was suddenly there; like a ghost, in her over large coat.

"What do you want from me? I'm warning you, I know all about you…"

Intimidate the enemy. A tactic that sometimes worked… with the suppliers. The young woman seemed at a loss for words.

"If it's Jacques Sergent you're looking for – or should I say Casimir de Claret-Llobet? – he isn't here."

"Claret-Llobet? Of course not. He's been dead for a long time!"

My God! They had found him and killed him. Now they had come for her. In fact, the hand of the Chinese woman had moved to her pocket… The pistol!

"Aaahhh! Help!" she screamed and threw the trolley and the bin towards the enemy. A noise like the roll of a drum resonated on the road way. Mademoiselle Pah avoided the missiles and fled, her limp grotesquely accentuated by her running. An object fell out of her coat. The gun?

Lights came on and windows opened, sleepy and unhappy faces appeared. One in particular, on the fourth floor: "You've become completely mad!" shrieked a livid Madame Belval.

Saving her job as well as her skin would have been too much to ask for. Resigned, Léonie went and picked up the pistol. Incredibly, when she bent over the object, she discovered that it was nothing more than a seed dibber.

Chapter 40

LEBLANC WAS LIVING on the other side of town in a big house surrounded by trees on a mound known as the Hill of the White Cloud.

"Monsieur has gone out," the maid answered when Bouillon knocked at the door.

"Where's he gone? It's urgent…"

She did not know. Bouillon dashed to Customs and Excise. If the theft of the opium had been noticed, this is where his boss and Ambroggiani must have come. The area around the building was deserted and the main entrance appeared hermetically sealed. Bouillon knocked. Nobody came to the door; an ominous sign. The guards should have reacted… The burglars might have killed them. He decided to go around the premises. A small door at the back was ajar, its lock forced. Bouillon did not go in but rushed to the Indigenous Guard post.

"Commander Ambroggiani, quickly!"

"Not here, gone on patrol."

On patrol? Was it in connection with the theft? Undecided, Emile headed towards The Travellers. There was nobody there. The Administrator General's garden-parties had done nothing for the local restaurant trade. In the mornings, people saved their hunger and in the evenings, they had sufficiently stuffed themselves for free so as not to need another meal. Vallée was alone at the bar.

"Hello stranger!" he said loudly. Didn't see you at the 4th July celebrations. Were you ill?"

"Not at all."

"You didn't miss much… What can I get you?"

"Nothing. Ambroggiani isn't here, is he?"

"As you can see…"

"Leblanc hasn't been either?"

"No. But this afternoon, because he didn't see you at the celebrations, he was worried… I think he even went over to your place."

Bouillon not being able to hold it in any longer, pulled the box of opium out of his haversack and placed it on the bar.

"Bloody hell! What are you doing with this?"

"Today I was at the loco. She was packed full of this stuff!"

"Are you kidding me?"

"Twenty crates or more. The entire stock of Customs and Excise."

"My God! Who could have done such a thing?"

Emile opened his hand to reveal the Hatamen butt.

"I also found this near Eliane. Doesn't it ring a bell?"

Vallée furrowed his brow.

"Claret-Llobet! Don't you remember? He was smoking these cigars all day long."

"Good Lord!"

"He's been hanging about in every nook and cranny of Guang-Zhou-Wan. He must have heard that Eliane had been exiled into the jungle and straight away saw his chance. She's half way to the Chinese border, he can safely keep the opium in the furnace before transferring it to the other side. Easy, since nobody ever goes that way."

"You do."

"On Sundays. Claret-Llobet must have also been told about it. Bad luck for him I went today, otherwise his timing was good. He probably acted during the night of the 13th to the 14th. With the National Day celebrations, no one was supposed to go back to work before the morning of the 15th. He would have needed what? About ten strong guys; five to overpower the guards, empty the refinery and move the opium to Eliane, five more to transship from there to China. They will probably do that tonight. If we hurry…"

"Afternoon, gentlemen!"

Surprised, Emile and Gabriel turned around. Ambroggiani was standing in the door of The Travellers, accompanied by three of his men.

"Ah! Ambro, hello…"

"Can I ask what you are hiding there?"

The commander of the indigenous Guard was looking at the box in Gabriel's hands.

"It's opium," replied Emile. I found it this afternoon in my locomotive."

"Really?"

"He's been looking everywhere for you to let you know!" stressed Gabriel.

"Look boys, enough of the hogwash. Anyone looking for me can find me. I've just come from Customs and Excise. Leblanc summoned me there, almost an hour ago. What a mess, there! A door was smashed, the guards were knocked out and tied up, and last but not least: the opium had disappeared, vanished, evaporated. And as if by magic, what do I spy here?"

"Exactly!" remarked Vallée. "We even know who did it: Claret-Llobet! Emile found a cigar butt next to the locomotive… a Hatamen. The brand the bastard smoked."

Bouillon had put away his exhibit, realizing that it did not have any value. A cigar butt could have been found anywhere, at any time and Ambroggiani was likely to say that. Moreover he did not seem interested in it. The intense contractions on his temples and his neck showed that he was pondering his next response. It was cutting:

"Bouillon, we haven't seen you all day whereas, until now, you've never missed a 14th of July. As for you, Vallée, I catch you with your paws on the loot, and you, he barked at Wawa whom he had just seen spying from the kitchen, I know you... You are going to come down to the station where you'll be able to repeat, at your pleasure, all the stories which might pass through your head, Claret-Llobet and more."

Despite the late hour, teams of Chinese workers were busy taking down the flags in the streets. Ambroggiani was walking beside the prisoners, chest swelling, sure of himself. His subordinates were following just behind. Almost there, they could already make out the sentry boxes of the Indigenous Guard.

On their left, very close, the worksite of a new residential area, abandoned since the beginning of the war. A peasant woman suddenly exited the site, pushing a fully loaded cart. Planks, bricks, iron rods, etc; booty, doubtless, stolen from there. At the sight of the uniforms, she began a U-turn but did not go through with it: the manoeuvre too much resembled an escape. Instead, she marched on steadily, determined to cross the street right under the eyes of the soldiers.

"Hey! Bouillon!"

Emile dashed off, knocking over the woman and her stuff. Ambroggiani and his men tried to go around the obstacle. But the woman on the ground bleated out that she was being attacked. She grabbed the trousers of the commander of the Indigenous Guard. He shook his leg to make her let go. She screamed even louder. He pulled out his service weapon and shot in the air. The woman clinging onto his ankles became even more furious. Until suddenly...

"Where has he gone, the bastard? I swear, he won't get very far."

Chapter 41

"SO, THE CHINESE woman paid you a visit?"

Léonie had called Fleurus, on the stringent directive of her husband.

"It happened at around five o'clock in the morning... I was putting the dustbins out."

"So early?"

"I couldn't sleep."

"Something was troubling you?"

"Not exactly... Perhaps I had a kind of premonition."

"Pre - mo - ni - tion?"

Salsify regurgitated the word slowly, as if it belonged to a foreign dialect he did not understand. Léonie thought for a moment that she was in a dialogue from the radio's *Masters of Mystery*.

"It's stupid," she admitted.

"But, in the end, this girl what did she want from you?"

"It's difficult to explain..."

"Did she threaten you?"

"Not exactly. How shall I put it...?"

Mademoiselle Pah had not said or done anything hostile. Moreover, what she was hiding under her coat was not a pistol but a stupid garden tool, which Léonie thought it wise not to show to the police inspector.

"I asked her if she was after Monsieur Sergent, she answered no, and added that he was dead. They've killed him!"

The policeman wrinkled his brow.

"Five in the morning... A good time for a house-breaking. Sergent out of the way? The Chinese woman was perhaps coming to search his apartment. It would be good if I could have a look in there myself. Have you got a master-key? I'll touch nothing and put everything back in its place."

Léonie did not comment on the contradiction: in Sergent's flat, there was essentially nothing to touch and therefore little to put back in its place. She acceded to Fleurus' request; wasn't she herself curious to see him at work?

The place smelt musty. Léonie aired whilst the policeman began his investigation. Indeed, he was hardly touching anything. His pale eyes were vainly searching for something to fix his attention on. The lounge, the bedroom, even the kitchen… deserts, almost unfurnished.

"That's a safe, isn't it?" Salsify had at last found a bone to chew. "Of course, if he's got anything, it'll be in there."

Not the fastest out of the gate! The caretaker gave a slight smile. The inspector did a circuit around Sergent's desk on which lay a pile of old *Figaro* newspapers. He looked surprised to find that the drawers opened without a key. In the left hand drawer, bills for the flat: gas, electricity, water, telephone, etc. In the right, stationery: writing paper, envelopes, pens, staples, scissors… Plus a small bottle of cough syrup. Fleurus opened it and smelt its contents. Association of ideas? He headed towards the bathroom.

"I'm going to inspect the medicine cabinet."

Léonie started to flick through the *Figaros*. The oldest ones dated from the beginning of the year. Strange how some events seemed already remote, almost incoherent. 'European Economic Community Comes Into Being' ran the headline of 1st January. Who cared nine months later? And 'Submarine Nautilus Goes Under North Pole's Pack Ice.' Bully for it! One day, wouldn't we land on the moon?

As a matter of fact: 'Americans Launch Explorer Satellite.' Six months after the Russians and their Sputnik, and before God knows who. 'Fangio Kidnapped by the Cubans.' They had since liberated him. 'Algiers: Military Take Over Power.' De Gaulle had quickly got rid of them. 'World Cup Starts Tomorrow in Sweden.' That, she wouldn't forget for a long time. For three long weeks Ernest had been pestering her with his football matches, and that wasn't all. With his mates from the printing house, he had been to Bourget airport to cheer the French team on their return from Stockholm. And how had he managed, he being so clumsy, to obtain autographs from Fontaine and Marche? In twenty years, he would still boast about his exploit. The following issue would undoubtedly have several columns devoted to the opening match, Germany vs. Argentina, 3-2 to the Germans, which had made her husband moan so much: "The *Mannschaft*, whaooo! Heavier than a Panzer division!"

Oh… Léonie was disappointed not to be able to check her forecast. The *Figaro* of 8th June was not open at its front page. Nor were the following ones… She had to wait until the 29th to find a front page in place. 'Brazil Defeats Sweden 5-2 Wins World Cup. France, an Excellent Third.' Was Sergent thinking of moving out? All the issues from 8 to 28 were open at the property ads. He had circled some in red. They were all stylish properties located in respectable suburbs of Paris: Vaucresson, Ville d'Avray, Chatou, Versailles or even…

"Jesus Christ!"

"What is it?"

Fleurus forgetting the broom cupboard, the existence of which he had just discovered, came closer.

"Just this…"

The caretaker pointed to the adverts, but studiously ignored one:

Rambouillet, rue de la Motte, fully renovated mansion, 8 rooms, kitchen, bathroom, cellar, garage, park of 3,000 m2. Price, 10 million, negotiable. Tel. Opéra 5721, any day, 09:00 to 20:00

"May I? It seems that you have hit the jackpot... I tip my hat to you Madame Burot! If Sergent bought one of these houses, we'll soon know about it."

The inspector conscientiously wrote down all the adverts encircled in red in his notebook. Léonie contented herself with memorising *Opéra 5721*.

Chapter 42

THE MORNING DEW was pearling into droplets along the rows of vegetables in their garden. Pah was weeding between the aubergines, the seeds of which they had bought together at the market three months earlier.

"It's me," murmured Bouillon in order not to frighten her.

She stopped her work and looked him up and down. He realised he looked quite pitiable.

"You spent the night in the jungle?"

She did not seem to know what had happened. It was still early but hadn't Henriette, whose husband had been arrested, broadcast it to everyone in Fort-Bayard?

"Henriette? No I haven't seen her. But your boss came by, yesterday afternoon. Since apparently you had promised him you would attend the festivities, he thought you were sick. I reassured him telling him that you had gone to visit your locomotive."

Bouillon went into the house, where she followed him.

"Could you make me a coffee?"

He was staring at the coffee pot on the gas. It was not boiling fast enough to his liking. He switched it up.

"Sorry, I'm in a bit of a hurry. I must go out again…"

"For your work?" she asked, doubtful. "Change your clothes at least…"

She was right. He should shower, shave, put on some clean clothes. Ambroggiani, though, could turn up at any minute. He stood by the window. The rare passersby did not even cast a glance at their house. Didn't they know?

"What is there to eat?"

She opened the food cupboard; almost empty. Eggs, a chunk of bread, sausages, some fruit.

"I haven't been to the shops yet."

"Can you do me some eggs?"

"Hard, soft, fried?"

"Hard, unless…"

He was wondering, like for the coffee, how long they'd take.

"Do you want them or not?"

He nodded. She filled a saucepan with water and put it in the place of the coffee pot.

"There's something wrong?"

"No."

Why was he unable to confide in Pah? Wasn't she the being he cherished most, his daughter?

He drank his coffee and decided to go and wash. The cold water he splashed on his face, the fire of the razor, even the clean vest sliding over his skin, all produced a sensation of revival. And if he were to find Claret-Llobet? A plan was starting to take shape in his mind. He could, as early as this evening, go to Customs and Excise and look for clues. He would then return to Eliane. The opium, he couldn't hope to lay his hands on again, but the thief and his accomplices may have left behind more than just the cigar.

"Your eggs are ready."

"I'll take them with me…"

Just like the rest of the food which he shoved into his bag.

"I'll be back soon. Have you got enough money for the week?"

He gave her a kiss before leaving.

A visit to the Customs and Excise warehouse, to Eliane

in the jungle? As soon as he was outside, in the oppressive heat, this program seemed unfeasible to him. All of a sudden he felt like returning home and waiting, with Pah at his side, for them to come and interrogate him. Fleeing wouldn't be a way out. Nevertheless, he set off, with no other goal than to leave the town where someone would be sure to spot him. He reached the foothills of the Mandarin. This bare mountain peak dominated Fort-Bayard, giving the town some shade. There was an abandoned cabin at the top. Why not rest there?

The path climbed from the salt marshes which local people had been exploiting for ages past, long before the arrival of the French. He passed close by the workers who were raking the pans. They were puffing and panting, the salt and the sun creasing their skin and they would probably not finish work before night fall. But didn't they form a team, a family, in solidarity with their rites, their traditions, their rules? He, on the other hand, had brutally cut himself off from the world and could see no way to get back. He resumed his climb, fatigued, desperate.

The whirling winds which whipped the summit had polished it like the bald head of a Buddha on which the cabin formed an ugly mole. Down below, Fort-Bayard stretched dull and unattractive, but in front of him, perhaps two kilometers away, as the crow flies, was the green and pleasant Hill of the White Cloud. A red roof here and there burst through its luxuriant canopy.

That was where his boss resided. The day before he had not been able to see him, and without doubt one could easily see that that was the main cause of his current predicament. If he could just tell him his story, calmly, rationally, wouldn't the man believe him and testify in his favour?

That's it! he became excited. Tonight, he would go to neither Customs and Excise nor to the Surprise but to see Leblanc and talk to him.

Chapter 43

WITH FLEURUS HAVING gone, Léonie rushed to dial *Opéra 5721*.

"Hello, I'm calling about the advert in the *Figaro*. The house in Rambouillet…"

"It was sold a long time ago" answered a lady with a rather gruff voice.

Duly noted. But could she possibly make this lady reveal the name of the buyer?

"It interests us very much, my husband and me… Might the new owner be persuaded to sell it on for a small profit?"

"I would be very surprised…"

"Why might that be?"

"The buyer is not so harebrained. He wouldn't sell straight away to the first fool who comes along," the old lady derided. "As a matter of fact, it wasn't an individual but a company. Foreign, even, from Luxembourg."

"From Luxembourg? Oh! OK, never mind then," capitulated Léonie.

"I can't remember the name exactly, I'd have to check in my papers…"

"No thank you, it's not necessary."

"A commercial enterprise anyway," continued her correspondent without listening to her. "And even international. Something to do with Asia…"

"I beg your pardon?"

At that point Léonie wished that the lady would just go and get the bill of sale.

"Yes. The Commercial Enterprise for Europe and Asia, or something like that."

"And do you also remember the director, I mean the person who signed the bill at the notary public's office?"

"The representative? A charming man. And he didn't argue about the price. Before him, I had to put up with all sorts…"

Between the *skinflints* who wanted to dispossess her for peanuts, the fussy ones who insisted on brand new washers for all the taps, the *under-the-table* types and the *maybe-yes, maybe-no* ones with whom she would still have been dealing even now…

"I have no time for those kinds of people. So I can tell you that I went for this man straight away. Serious, honest, confident, a rarity these days…

The description matched the man from 3rd floor, Flat C, but one shouldn't rush to conclusions.

"A Luxembourger?"

"No. A Frenchman."

"Was his name Jacques Sergent, by any chance?"

"It was. How do you know? And in fact, the name of the company is coming back to me: EEAC, Enterprise for Euro-Asian Commerce"

"And in Luxembourg, you said."

"Yes, but they have an office in Paris. This too I remember perfectly well because, believe it or not, it's located in my old neighbourhood, number 14 avenue Velasquez, close to Parc Monceau."

Chapter 44

L EBLANC OPENED the door himself this time.
"You?" He looked his employee up and down, like Pah
had done that morning, then, briskly, pulled him by the
sleeve. "Don't stand on the step. If someone were to see
you…"

A lobby with pearl grey wall hangings, a panelled
staircase and a sweetish odour, an undefinable mixture of
provincial France and ancient China.

"Let's go upstairs…" A vast lounge; beige leather
armchairs, ebony bookshelves sheltering chinaware and
antique statuettes, a massive table with legs ending in claw
feet. Emile had rather imagined his boss living in an open,
airy house with modern and bright coloured furniture, the
type for which one could sometimes see adverts for in
L'Asie Nouvelle, destined for executives in Indochina. *Equip
your home the Parisian way. Direct imports from France,
stylish and contemporary creations. Grandin Stores.* Or was it
Grandet, he couldn't remember.

"Sit down. Can I offer you something? A brandy, an eau-
de-vie?" The Director of Customs and Excise displayed
some elegant flasks in a secretaire.

"I don't know… whatever you're having."

"Brandy then, it'll perk you up. I have the impression you
need it."

The alcohol shimmered in the crystal glasses.

"… Cheers! Let's drink first, then you can tell me all
about your worries."

Worries! Typical of Leblanc. Polite and innocuous words
which reduced his case to the lot of the common man, to

191

the small annoyances of life, tomorrow he would feel better. Emile already regretted his move.

"Another one?"

His boss pointed to his glass, already empty. He had gulped down his brandy without even realizing it. He declined the offer and was effusive in his apologies, experiencing a strange sensation of being unsettled by his own voice. The alcohol was already having an effect on his exhausted state. Even Leblanc seemed strange to him. Calm and affable, he was patiently waiting for his visitor to start speaking, so like himself that he was no longer himself: just a mask, a caricature.

Emile's eyes fixed on a painting, a vertical scroll hanging on the wall. A lake, from which emerged, through a winter mist, scattered islets linked by frail bridges. Three figures, wrapped in warm clothes, furtively greeted each other, destined to soon disappear, swallowed up by the scenery. The whole swathed in tones of gray and brown, as if other colours, barely distinguishable, were also being swallowed up.

"Do you like it?"

The scene reminded Bouillon of the winters of his childhood, when he walked to school through frosted fields. A deep silence reigned, occasionally broken by the dull tapping of a peasant's hoe, or the hypnotizing caw of a crow.

"Chinese painting, one tires of it less quickly than of a pretty woman, and often gains better pleasure from it."

Leblanc was surely expressing himself figuratively, but what strange and, above all, previously unexpressed images coming from him! A revelation for Emile.

"My greatest pleasure doesn't reside in the viewing, but in the unrolling of the painting. You see this scroll... Closed up, what marvel will it reveal? An undressing in a way. I told you, as with a lady. And when you roll it back up? Even better! You don't see anything, you consent to the deprivation, you have to be content with the memory. Fundamentally, the more I'm captivated by a painting, the less I feel the need to see it. It's inside me, it impregnates my soul, forever…"

Yet didn't Emile, in the past, feel the same way whilst aboard the railway of the Little Belt? The scenery was living within him, he didn't have to look at it anymore. It's presence deep inside his being sufficed to make him happy. With this he was, astonishingly, discovering something in common with his boss.

"But I imagine that you didn't come to hear me expound on Art. Is it about opium?"

"Yes. Ambroggiani must have told you that they had arrested us, Vallée, Wawa and me, at The Travellers, with a stolen box…"

His story started well. He knew however that it would be difficult for him to finish it and keep it coherent. He would have appreciated it if Leblanc had interrupted him, asked him questions, but his host only listened to him silently.

"This opium I had found it in the afternoon in my locomotive… Entire crates in actual fact. You know that I often go there. Every Sunday generally speaking. Yesterday, the fancy took me to go there rather than to the 14th July celebrations. I know that you were expecting me there and that you were concerned about my absence. I apologize…"

Leblanc smiled with an indulgence which should have comforted Bouillon. On the contrary, it made him uncomfortable.

"Anyway, the firebox of my machine is full of opium. At least… Still doubting what I was seeing, I prised open a crate to check. It definitely was. I extracted a box, as proof. Back in Fort-Bayard, I looked for you and for the commandant of the Indigenous Guard. I couldn't find either of you. As a last resort, I went to The Travellers. I showed the box to Gabriel and Wawa... It was at that moment that Ambrioggiani nabbed us, because, in the mean time, you had discovered the theft and reported it."

Was it convincing? Leblanc swigged the last of his brandy.

"Personally, I'm only too pleased to believe you. As a matter of fact, you will have noticed that I've welcomed you into my home when I have every reason to curse the person or persons who did this, for it is clear that I will be disciplined..."

Bouillon showed astonishment.

"Of course, yes! See what happened to the previous Administrator General after the debacle of your train. For me, it'll be the same. This opium, I'm responsible for it. 'You didn't know how to look after it? Big mistake, Monsieur Leblanc. Good bye!' This is what they're going to say in Hanoi, and there is no means of appeal. But let's get back to you. I agree on one point: what interest might you have had in this theft? None. The thing is..."

"Yes, I know. I shouldn't have fled."

"I'm not talking about that. One gets confused, sometimes. But your friends..."

"My friends?"

"Gabriel Vallée and this Wawa... Haven't they ever told you about their dabbling in trafficking?"

Chapter 45

S HE WOULD HAVE preferred to proceed without delay to avenue Velasquez. However, any negligence in the upkeep of her own building risked playing into the hands of old Belval. So she got down to polishing the brasses, yet without exhausting herself, for was it worth putting in so much effort and setting such an example just for her? It would have meant paying too much attention to this infuriating woman. Being too mindful to the idiocy of the human race is pointless anyway... "It's like the flow of the Seine. When it goes up, it goes up. No barrier can stop it," philosophised Antoinette.

4:30. Abandoning her bannisters, Léonie went into the lodge to prepare her son's tea and the bottle of Picon bitters for Verger. They had got into this habit: every day the policeman would pick Frédéric up from school and bring him home.

4:45. Nobody.

5:00...

5:05...

5:10. What on earth were they doing? She was tempted to go and meet them. Yes but... if the school called, in the meantime, to explain their lateness, which had a cause no doubt... but what? Dark thoughts; she chased them away.

5:15. They were going to arrive: a question of minutes, seconds...

5:20. Her legs weakened. She sat down, got up again... her heart: boom, boom... Right, leave the lodge, go and see. Her keys... where had she put them? Impossible to think.

5:25. The hands of her clock went round more quickly than the wings of a windmill… "Stupid!" She should not be going out, she should telephone. Fleurus, the fire brigade, the…

"Hello mum!"

The door of the lodge opened wide and Frédéric, excited, rushed inside. Verger followed, out of breath.

"So sorry, Madame Burot…"

Léonie hugged her son.

"You really scared me! Did the teacher make you stay behind?"

She almost wished it.

"No! You'll never guess!"

"Tell me…"

"Try to guess!"

"I have no idea…"

"You give up?"

"Yes."

"Shall I tell her?"

Frédéric was alternatively looking at his mother and Verger who, by screwing up his eyes, gave his agreement.

"We've arrested the Chinaman!"

"My God!"

"It was me who recognized him. He was wearing different glasses and a beret and a pullover instead of his cap and anorak, but that didn't fool me. And you should have seen the way Raymond, I mean Monsieur Verger, grabbed him!"

The policeman kept his nose in his bitters. He knew these compliments wouldn't last long.

"But where, rue des Bauches? In front of the school?"

"Er… no. At Café Bilboquet."

Better tell your mother everything, or nearly everything

and not beat about the bush, Verger had advised Frédéric, for the incident had not passed unnoticed around them.

"What d'you mean Café Bilboquet? Which Café Bilboquet?"

"Ah, the café not far from the school. With monsieur Verger, we were drinking a lemonade, just after school. The Chinaman was there, spying on us."

Léonie looked daggers at Verger, who again looked deeply into his aperitif. Not only exposing a child to the debauchery of a bar, but also risking having him kidnapped, which was for sure the Chinaman's plan. How could one lack so much morality and common sense?

Fleurus arrived shortly afterwards. He had 'received' the suspect, who had been transferred to the Criminal Investigation Department.

"He doesn't have any papers and refuses to talk. No name, no address, no nothing. A tough one, but in the end he'll soften up."

His name? Wawa. His address? 1, rue Gambetta in Rambouillet. It would have been so easy for Léonie to pass on this precious information to the inspector. The gang was now after her son. Having them locked up was as necessary as stopping the Germans on the Marne, yet something was still holding her back.

"I'd like to ask you… Now we know that these people…"

"That these people what?"

"Are threatening us. Maybe we should be protected a bit better…"

Salsify looked at Verger scathingly – Léonie felt embarrassed for him – but his silent verdict was that, despite what people might think, this was a suitable bodyguard.

"The Chinaman is behind bars," recognized the caretaker, "but there remains…"

"The Chinese woman, I know. But what do you want? A cordon of policemen around your house?"

"Perhaps not going so far…"

"Good… we'll see what we can do…"

Ridiculously little backup against individuals she could have had imprisoned on the spot. Had she lost her reason? She had to accept that eventuality. The next morning, very early, she would go and see Pioux and his henchmen. Avenue Velasquez would have to wait. What would she say, what would she do to these mad and bloodthirsty creatures? Anger and supplication: had they been here, within her reach, would she have gouged out their eyes, and then immediately afterwards implored them not to attack her own flesh and blood?

Chapter 46

"THEIR DABBLING IN trafficking?" repeated Bouillon.

"Ah yes!" confirmed Leblanc with a jubilant nervousness. "Doesn't Wawa's father own a junk where he, as a matter of fact, put you up, in the past, you and Vallée, and doesn't The Travellers have a secluded and spacious cellar? A boat for transport, a hideout for illicit goods: a perfect set up for the casual smuggler…"

"But…"

"If I'm aware of all this, and have been for such a long time, why didn't I intervene? Let's say they amused me, your friends who thought they could fool me when their game was so naive and transparent… Amateurish. But if I were to lock up all the amateur traffickers in Fort-Bayard… Alas with hindsight, in the case of Vallée and Wawa, I think I should have. For, no doubt, you are not aware of the latest developments. This afternoon, Ambroggiani inspected the basement of The Travellers. And do you know what he discovered there? Not the usual trivia: alcohol or tobacco, but all sorts of guns and ammunition. If they are already involved in the smuggling of arms, then Vallée and his pet monkey are also perfectly capable of having stolen our opium… Don't you think so? Are you absolutely certain of their innocence?"

Bouillon still kept the Hatamen stub in his pocket. Why wasn't he showing it, nor claiming that its presence near Eliane represented if not proof, at least a serious indication of Claret-Llobet's involvement? No, even more than with Ambroggiani, the object seemed negligible, it was no proof at all.

"I don't doubt your sincerity. But try to think: your friends, couldn't they have subtly extorted information from you about the way one enters the warehouse? Not everyone knows that the back door leads almost directly to the storage room…"

These developments were so unexpected that Bouillon did not react.

"In any case, for them, it'll soon be a different story. A Japanese one…"

The Japanese? They were not the ones who meted out justice in Fort-Bayard. Emile did not understand. His superior explained:

"I should keep mum because the matter is still confidential, but you should know that France is going to return Guang-Zhou-Wan to the pro-Japanese Government of Nankin. The Administrator General is already negotiating the transfer of power. A whole battalion of Japanese will arrive in a short while. You can imagine that they'll prove to be less easy-going than the French Government of Indochina. Smuggling, trafficking, stealing, they won't tolerate any of that. Especially if it concerns arms and opium. You see, this theft at the warehouse, I can tell you that at the Japanese military mission they are not at all happy about it. Didn't you know that the government in Tokyo uses the drug as a weapon? That in Manchuria, their troops have planted poppies everywhere and addicted entire populations in order to render them docile? You can be sure that they were planning to lay their hands on our stock and use it for the same purpose. So, when Colonel Ito and his junta enjoy full power, the culprits, real or imagined, are going to pay, and dearly. I'm immensely sorry, but France shouldn't have lost the war!"

Leblanc's voice became tinged with aggressiveness.

Emile chose to take his leave.

"Where will you go?"

"I don't know…"

"Cross over to China and go to Tonkin. You have money?"

"No."

"Take this at least."

His boss took a wad of notes from his secretaire and slid it into Bouillon's bag. Groggy, he neither thought of refusing nor of saying thank you.

"I would have liked to suggest you spend the night here, but it would be too dangerous."

Emile found himself outside. Sleep. That was all he could think about.

Chapter 47

*T*O INSPECTOR FLEURUS,

I'm writing to inform you that as well as the Chinaman you arrested yesterday, I have identified and located the rest of the murderers of Antoinette Leroux. Right now, it would be too long to explain how. This morning, I'm going to tell them what I think and attempt to persuade them not to harm my little Frédéric, or any of my relatives. I'll make sure that I don't fall into their clutches. But if you find this note or if someone delivers it to you, it'll mean that something has gone wrong. Therefore, I'm writing here the address of the people I'm visiting: 'Jean Pioux – Flowering and Ornamental Plant Nursery', 1 rue Gambetta in Rambouillet. They are linked (the Ministry of Foreign Affairs' archives will provide you with more information) to the scandal of the railway in Fort-Bayard of which Jacques Sergent, under the name Casimir de Claret-Llobet, was the instigator.

Yours sincerely,

Léonie Burot, Paris, 27th September 1958.

Pioux, when opening the gate, looked more intrigued than hostile.

"Let me warn you, no tricks. I've left a letter for the police at home, in case…"

The horticulturist didn't respond to the warning. She followed him into the greenhouse. It was hot inside, stifling even. Guang-Zhou-Wan! She imagined herself there as if having stepped inside the photos. A big thermometer on the wall indicated 32 degrees Celsius.

The fan and the spray didn't bring any relief. On the contrary, they spread the humidity throughout the room and onto one's body. Sitting in the same places as the first time, the old man and Pah didn't seem to mind it. The climate must have been similar in the colony. This job which kept them continually in the heat suited them perfectly. And, when they had to go out... Pah's heavy coat, her fellow countryman's cap and anorak: heat-giving rather than camouflaging outfits.

"Your friend has been captured," she threw at them.

She watched for a reaction. There was none.

"He was spying on my son. You were planning to kidnap him, weren't you?"

Pioux breathed in deeply.

"Madame Burot, we tried first to telephone you, but we couldn't find your number..."

Of course not, the phone was in the name of the management committee. But what had the phone call to do with a kidnaping attempt? Mad people! She was dealing with mad people!

"... As a consequence you see, the telephone was not an option. Talking to you directly as Pah did the other morning? You got angry. Sending you a letter? You would have been most suspicious. That left us with only one possibility: to pass on our message via your son. Naive perhaps, but we are at the end of our tether..."

"Oh! What nonsense!"

And how about her, wasn't she at the end of her tether? And, passing on a message via Frédéric... What was this new fable? A message covered in poison, like the photographs? It was not kidnapping they were talking about, but murder!

"There is obviously a misunderstanding," continued Pioux.

"Oh yes? What misunderstanding?"

"Jacques Sergent."

Was Jacques Sergent a misunderstanding? One for which poor Antoinette had paid with her life. The horticulturist had the audacity…! Or was it a tactic? Come out with anything and everything in order to daze and confuse her! She was not just going to let it happen:

"You must have been tickled pink when you saw him wandering around Rambouillet a few months ago, looking for a house to buy. You had found Casimir de Claret-Llobet again, your old associate from the railway, who had robbed you twenty years ago and more over… You could at last take your revenge!

"I deduce, from what you say, that the police have not got hold of Wawa's document."

"Another fabrication of yours?"

"No. Without doubt the death of your friend motivates you to search for the truth. The document I'm talking about, our message, would have clearly revealed it…"

Pioux had hardly finished his sentence when he opened the drawer in his table.

The pistol! He was going to shoot her.

"Bastard!" she cursed in order to have the final word.

A clamour, a fall, a blow on the head… That's it, she was dead. Dead but, like Lazarus, resurrected. She opened her eyes again. Around her, angels in abundance, dressed in black uniforms and wearing kepis. Apart from the two non-uniformed Saints in whose arms she found herself… Peter and his assistant? Which shows that you can't judge a book by its cover: the assistant's face was covered with spots as profuse as a kid with chickenpox, and Saint Peter looked remarkably like Inspector Fleurus.

Chapter 48

SLEEP, BUT WHERE? Emile didn't think he had the strength to climb the Peak of the Mandarin again: it was too far, too high. He set off, hoping that an idea would come to him, that a shelter might materialize. His footsteps gradually led him towards Pointe Nivet. Was it Wawah's father's junk that was drawing him, which Leblanc had reminded him of? Not really. The Indigenous Guard was probably watching it. But he could perhaps find some other empty boat or even a bunk in the village. And the next day, with the money that Leblanc had given him, which he had not counted but which seemed to him a tidy sum, he would negotiate a crossing to China with the fishermen.

He had almost arrived at Pointe Nivet when he heard a jingle. Almost immediately, at the end of the road, a shape emerged out of the night: a horse and carriage. He jumped into the nearest thicket. As the carriage reached him, he saw it was pulled by a bay horse with a braided mane trotting along at a leisurely pace. A coachman and two passengers. The first, a Chinaman, was wrapped in a plain cloak from which his face protruded, with staring eyes as hard as stone, and two massive, brick-red hands. He had never met the man before, but how could he not recognize Seng Loon-Fat, the Lobster, the deposed opium refiner of Fort-Bayard? The second traveller was a small European man with curly hair and cheeks overgrown with side whiskers from another era. Emile knew him, he had come across him at Customs and Excise during a visit some years earlier: Dos Santos, the Farmer General of Macau!

The carriage disappeared into the dark, Bouillon remained in his bush until he could no longer hear it. First Casimir's cigar, and now Seng and Dos Santos going discreetly into town after visiting Pointe Nivet... The malfeasant three-man team first named by the Oliveira twins was therefore not just tittle-tattle, and their intentions were becoming clear: not to distribute the Lobster's opium in Chongqing, as Pioux had first believed, but, much more efficiently, seize the Customs and Excise's opium in Fort-Bayard. Leblanc was simply a fool, he hadn't seen anything coming and was falsely accusing Gabriel and Wawa of the crime.

Emile retraced his steps, following in the tracks of the carriage. He did not have to go very far. At the crossroads to Fort-Bayard and Tche-Kam, a tea house was still open, parked in front of it was the carriage. The coachman had joined a rowdy table outside, where swearwords led to roars of laughter. The Lobster and the Farmer General were not to be seen. They must have gone inside; one could only perceive silent shadows against the oilpaper covering the windows. Bouillon couldn't quite believe the situation. Although Pah and he must have passed the tea house every time they went to Tche-Kam, he hardly remembered it. To find it in the middle of the night filled with an animated and ebullient throng, didn't this look like an illusion?

Three men finally came out, conversing cordially. They were smoking cigars. Cigars with a royal blue ring, the overabundant smoke of which cocooned them in an ash coloured aura, just like merry devils.

Chapter 49

"JUST A SMALL bump on the head. The plants suffered more than you…"

Salsify showed Léonie the shelf she had knocked over in falling. Then pushing Pioux out of the way, he fully opened the drawer.

"Aha!" he remarked jeeringly while feeling the weight of the pistol he found there. "A beautiful pre-war German Mauser! You have a license?"

One could sense that he doubted it very much. Claret-Llobet's ex-associate did not bother to answer.

"…Your papers?"

Here too, the inspector was betting that he was dealing with citizens acting outside the law, but Pioux presented him with an identity card.

"Jean Lucien Pioux, born 4th April 1895 in Hanoi… h'mm… You're French?"

"As you can see. My mother was Annamese, if that's what bothering you."

"And you?" Fleurus addressed Bouillon.

Pah intervened. "Here are my papers and my father's."

"Your father?"

"Adoptive."

"Ah? Let's have a look. Emile Albert Bouillon, born 25th January 1900 in Carpiquet… Nicole Bouillon, given name Pah, born 2nd March 1923 in Guang-Zhou-Wan. We must check this."

"Check! Check? Leave us alone, free our friend and instead you'd better take care of that bastard!"

"I beg your pardon?"

Flabbergasted, Fleurus seemed uncertain about how he was going to put this dissident in her place.

"You heard very well what I said!"

"Take it easy! 'That bastard'… who are you talking about?"

"Are you stupid or what?"

"Miss, don't use that tone of voice with me!"

Léonie too was showing some impatience. The Chinese woman was right of course: the policeman was on the wrong track. As incredible as it may seem, it was not the murderers who were falsifying their identity, but their target. Because he was here, the inspector should have understood this, since he must have read her note.

"Take away the gun," he ordered 'spotty face' who had remained unnoticed, "and all the rest of the mess in this drawer. I can see some letters, some old documents in there…"

Then, to Léonie:

"It looks as if we've arrived just in time, haven't we, Madame Burot? A little later and this man would have shot you."

The caretaker forced a smile. Things were about to get worse for her, so she might as well consider the situation philosophically.

"You're not asking yourself how I happen to be here?" went on the inspector.

"My note?"

"Your note?"

"The one I left at home before I went out this morning, in which I informed you that I was coming here…

"No."

Léonie was thinking.

"Their letter, then…?"

Salsify ground his teeth. The caretaker and her letters – hers, theirs, clearly everybody was writing – was spoiling his moment.

"Apparently this Wawa, the Chinaman who was arrested yesterday, was in possession of a document, according to Monsieur Pioux…"

"No. Nothing was found on him either. *Me*, I am here, thanks to Bricoux…"

Fleurus paternally smiled at the acned young man whose face turned pink at the sound of his name.

"Bricoux and the classified adverts of *Le Figaro*… I too telephoned their contributors and managed to reach the seller of the house in Rambouillet…"

Léonie bit her lip. When calling *Opéra 5721*, she had indeed thought there might be a risk that Fleurus would also talk to the old lady. She had decided to do it anyway.

"You're not an easy act to follow. I felt the sharp end of her tongue, the lady who answered: 'I'm not an information centre! Why don't you ask the woman who just called me? I told her everything in the minutest detail! Who bought the house? Why don't you go to the Land Registry. Good bye!' Word for word. I then said to myself: 'You've got competition in this inquiry.' Who? You of course, since you had discovered the property sales pages at Sergent's. But one detail still bothered me: had you also contacted the other advertisers? I phoned them all. No, nobody before me had called Chatou, Vaucresson, Ville d'Avray or anywhere. Therefore you had not acted at random. You knew there was a link between Sergent and Rambouillet. The moment I understood you were playing a game, I decided to keep a close watch on you. The arrest of the Chinaman yesterday happened at just the right moment. You asked for a reinforced guard? I appointed Bricoux, giving him an extra task: to tail you. He spent the night in his car, a few metres from your place. When he saw you going out this morning, he followed you…"

My God! Léonie hadn't noticed anything. The young cop had really done his job well.

"Thank you," she said to him, thinking that he had probably saved her life.

From pink, his face turned bright red.

"Right," declared Fleurus. "It's exceedingly hot here. Everyone down to the CID! It'll be cooler there and we'll think better."

"And on what grounds?" reacted the horticulturist.

"Murder and attempted murder, prohibited carrying of a gun, amongst other things."

Pioux, haughtily, held his wrists out to be handcuffed.

Chapter 50

A N INSECT TICKLING the corner of his mouth; a ray of sunlight on his right, forcing his eyelids to close; a window with translucent curtains from which he turns his blinded eyes; a white ceiling with a softer light; a slow fan between the blades of which a fly is buzzing, undoubtedly the one that has just left his lips; four walls, a door, all equally white; an empty iron bed next to him, whose cream paint is peeling off; finally himself, lying flat in a similar bed. Why on earth was he in a hospital, his upper body and his head, encased in plaster?

"You're at last waking up!"

The deep voice coming from the direction of the door made him jump. A sharp pain made him wince. He choked back a cry and lay immobile, his mouth wide open. The visitor came closer. A face appeared in his field of vision, and a breath smelling of garlic in his field of smell: Ambroggiani.

"All I can say is that you made us run the other night."

"The o...ther...night?" The pain was lessening but Emile was experiencing a new handicap. He was having great difficulty articulating; he could almost feel the painful journey of his words from his brain to his lips.

"Don't pretend you don't remember. Near the ice factory, when we caught you."

What was the Commander of the Indigenous Guard saying to him? Searching his memory hurt and did not lead anywhere.

"... And you started to run like a man possessed, can't you remember that? And you wanted to cut through the fields? And that was a bad move since you ended up at the bottom of a pit? You're not a pretty sight right now…"

Yes perhaps he could see himself falling into a kind of giant sinkhole with black and rough sides. A fall with no beginning and no end; a dream: what could he have been doing near the ice factory?

"I've been… here… for a… long time?" he asked, feeling as though he were pulling a bucket full of water from a deep well.

"Two days. And I'm letting you know: the doctor has said that you are out of sorts and not well enough to be questioned. So, today, I'm only staying five minutes. But don't think that you're going to be able to play sick forever! In any case, we have new evidence against you…"

An oration in Double Dutch could not have been more discordant to Emile's ears.

"The cash we found in your bag. Three thousand piastres! Admit that you had started to sell the stuff, you rascal."

Three thousand piastres? That was absurd! He never kept more than five hundred in his purse; for fear of losing them or having them stolen… And the stuff, what stuff? The more the other heaped details upon him the less he understood.

"And let me tell you one more thing: one of you coming back, one of you on the way out…"

A rather obscure turn of phrase which Ambroggiani explained, a vicious glow in his eyes:

"Your friend Vallée… he hanged himself in his prison cell last night."

Gabriel, hanged in his cell? The joke was not at all good, and Ambroggiani was a disgrace. Emile gave up and fell asleep again.

When he woke up, a man with a bald head was bending over him. He was wearing a white coat on the lapel of which a name was sewn: Dr. Saunier.

"You've suffered a fracture of the skull and an injury to your spine. Do you understand?"

Bouillon nodded despite the plaster. His performance seemed to amaze the doctor who pulled a thermometer case out of his pocket.

"What colour is it?"

"Green."

"Fine. You can speak a little and your senses seem to function. You fell into a pit. Do you remember this?"

A veil of despair fell over the former railwayman.

"… Don't worry! We're going to get you back on your feet!"

Chapter 51

LÉONIE WOULDN'T HAVE swapped her lodge for Salsify's cubby-hole at the CID; not enough light and what sad looking furniture! Were the steel cupboard with one door missing and the office chair with only one arm the remains of a fire sale? Judging from these, the detainees were probably rotting at the bottom of a deep dungeon. Brr...

"Inspector Bergeron... Madame Burot..."

Another surprise was the presence of the man Bergeron, secluded in a corner of the room. He was typing out a report. He barely looked up and mumbled a bonjour. Fleurus invited Léonie to sit down. The mutilated chair leaned gently, despite a folded piece of cardboard which was supposed to stabilise it.

She decided to change neither her position nor her strategy: sit very still, say amen to everything, or almost everything, get it over with as quickly as possible and get home before her husband – who finishes work early on Saturdays. Should Ernest discover her note, it would be just about the limit! A low profile therefore, at least after making sure of the following:

"This Wawa had really no document on him?"

"I've told you! No document, no paper and hardly enough money to buy himself a sandwich. Pioux was having you on..."

"You think so? Why?"

Exhaling loudly, Fleurus explained that the brain of a crook functioned in an often obscure manner... but that his struggled to come up with an explanation for 'why'.

"Madame Burot, does your work bore you?" he started, on what he thought was safe ground.

Although Léonie more or less guessed what he was driving at, she feigned amazement:

"What on earth makes you think that!"

"I'm under the impression that you're tempted by police work, and that right from the beginning of this case, you wanted to play the investigator and sweep away all those who didn't let you: the journalist for example, and me, to a certain extent…"

"Not at all!"

"Come off it! I don't know what your reasons might be but look where it almost led you: in Rambouillet, admit that that was close."

The shaky 'yes' she conceded got lost in a burst from Bergeron's Japy.

"Let's forget about it. Let's talk rather about Interpol: the international police, if you like, for it will not have escaped your attention that the case has an international dimension; so Interpol, whom I have kept informed, passed on my questions to their colleagues in Hong Kong…"

"Excellent," she said flatteringly.

He opened his exercise book.

"I wanted particularly to know who, over there, was capable of producing or possessing lewisite and etorphine, both of the poisons spread over the photographs sent to Sergent. This is their reply…

Lewisite: Japanese stocks from Second World War discovered in Canton, controlled by Kuomintang then communists; officially destroyed in 1950 but probably stolen.

Etorphine: no laboratory has means to refine it in Hong Kong. Official importations tightly controlled; for veteri-

nary use; minimal quantities; clandestine production very difficult; only one or two traffickers proficient, among whom Seng Loon-Fat..."

Ending his telegraph, his eyes fixed on Léonie's.

"Seng Loon-Fat," he encanted. "According to Interpol, this fellow rose to fame under the French, in Fort-Bayard."

"Mother of God!" That swine Belval had hit the nail on the head by establishing a parallel with the Canut affair. Pioux and his accomplices, spotting Sergent in Rambouillet, had undoubtedly employed this poisoner, an old friend from their life over there, to prepare and send the poisoned letter.

"I also have confirmation that Jacques Sergent lived in the colony..."

"It was to be expected," the caretaker said carefully, playing down what she had known for a long time.

"Except that he was doing an unusual job: entrepreneur of railways; it's true he did so under a pseudonym: Casimir de Claret-Llobet... do you know how I learned this crucial fact?"

"You said Interpol," answered Léonie somewhat arrogantly, who had not needed the 'international police' to reach the same conclusion.

"Not at all. I simply went to the Record Office of the Ministry of Foreign Affairs..."

She seethed inside. Fleurus was lying, since she knew from Philibert that he had been rebuffed.

"I consulted the file on Fort-Bayard. Very informative. Look..."

The caretaker immediately identified the yellowish document with the purple text, which Salsify showed her: the carbon copy which the archivist had, he assured her, an exclusive view of! The only possible explanation: this wretched man had played a double game. Because she had not succumbed to his ridiculous advances, straight after his visit to rue François Ponsart, he must have made his way to the CID.

"Everything is in this letter. Read it."

She pretended to do so.

"Informative, as you say. I now understand better why monsieur Sergent was avoiding the police."

"Pff… He didn't run that big a risk. Fraud, in our country, lapses after five years…"

"Really? In other words he has nothing to fear from the justice system?"

"For that business with the railway, no, but perhaps there are other skeletons in his cupboard?"

It might be a good idea if there were! If five years were enough for a crook to hide himself from justice… Didn't the impunity of the man from third floor, flat C, give his pursuers some good reasons for pursuing him?

"By the way," said Salsify coming out of a train of thought of his own, "the house in Rambouillet… the old lady, did she tell you whether Sergent had bought it from her in the end? Because, to me, *Niet*!"

Poor Fleurus, sent back by the Record Office and ill-treated by his witnesses! Didn't he merit a little help from her, for once?

"Yes," she answered soberly.

Only partly true since the real buyer was EEAC. But hadn't she better keep one step ahead?

"Thank you."

The policeman got up and held out his hand. Somewhat surprised that he should set her free so easily, Léonie hesitated then held out hers. The telephone interrupted their next move. They sat down again. Salsify picked up.

Chapter 52

S AUNIER REAPPEARED, accompanied by a new character. "This gentleman wishes to have a word with you. I have decided that your state will allow it. I'll leave you both to it…"

"Do you recognize me? I am Judge Ferret, from the territory's tribunal. We've already met, in other circumstances…"

True, the man occasionally came to Customs and Excise to talk with Leblanc about current inquiries into smuggling. But why was he coming to see Bouillon?

"Well. You know what you're being accused of? Of having, on 14th July with your accomplices, Gabriel Vallée and the young Chinaman called Wawa, perpetrated the theft of twenty-two crates of opium: the entire stock of Customs and Excise."

Although preposterous, Ferret's allegations nevertheless explained those made by Ambroggiani. The opium was undoubtedly the 'stuff' which he accused him of having started to sell.

"National… Day? I must have… attended the celebra…"

"No."

Why couldn't he remember any of his actions on that particular day? He wasn't even able to place it exactly in terms of time, and even less to link it with his present state. As if a piece of his existence had been deleted, or transformed into an opaque and impenetrable hotchpotch.

"Vallée is, sadly, dead, so there are only two of you left to answer…"

"What?"

"He hanged himself yesterday in his cell. I thought the commander of the Indigenous Guard had informed you…"

"Hanged… for… what?"

"Guilt, remorse… This should help you to think."

To think? Bouillon was trying. But he was overcome by the confirmation of Gabriel's death. His mind was as agitated as a wasp in a glass of wine whose efforts to stay afloat hasten its drowning.

"Now, you're going to listen to me carefully," continued the magistrate. "Gabriel Vallée and Wawa were also in the business of smuggling arms. We have found a lot in the cellar at The Travellers. Were you involved in this?"

Silence from Emile. Ferret did not pursue the matter.

"According to Vallée, you discovered the opium in your locomotive, which you visited on 14th July. Do you maintain this fact?"

"I… don't… know, I…"

"If it's supposed to be an alibi, it is most futile. This piece of machinery not being endowed with speech, makes it difficult for me to collect a testimony. Unless someone saw you… Your friends moreover have asserted that near the locomotive you had found the butt of a cigar, the brand of which was apparently favoured by your former employer, Casimir de Claret-Llobet and that from this you would infer his guilt. Allow me to describe this hypothesis as frivolous. First of all believe me, if Claret-Llobet had again shown his face in Fort-Bayard, he would have been spotted… and arrested because I have for a long time issued several warrants against him. Besides, it's not the cigar butt – and actually, where is it? – which will prove anything. I too smoke cigars, like a lot of people here! Anyway, Ambroggiani went there, to your locomotive, as early as 15th July to tell you the truth. She was empty. The only trace of opium that we've found so far was on you. As well as the three thousand piastres, which gives credence to your involvement…"

Emile frowned. His locomotive, Eliane, yes, he remembered her, and their Sundays together. He remembered Claret-Llobet too: his eccentric outfits, his Hatamens which, it's true, he took great pleasure in, his witty repartees and his embezzlement. But he no more understood the theft of the opium than he did the irruption of Eliane and of Casimir and his cigars into the story. His mind wandered to other things: his encounter with Pah in the brothel, the dress and the slippers he offered after buying her, Henriette, her delicious cuisine and her affectations with Wawa; wouldn't she be inconsolable on the death of her husband? What secret pain had been tormenting Gabriel? Could it just have been Ferret's insane accusations that caused him to hang himself? No! His friend wasn't that easily influenced.

Chapter 53

"IT'S VERGER," announced Fleurus covering the mouth piece. "What? At the school? We are coming straight away!"

"Frédéric?" anguished Léonie.

"Yes... He has found a suspicious letter in his satchel."

"My God! The message from the Chinaman! And did he...?"

"No. Don't worry, nobody touched it. Your son himself thought it was suspicious and informed his teacher."

Salsify kept the phone in his hand and dialed a number.

"Hello, Dr. Beaumont? It's Fleurus. We've just been notified about an envelope. Probably from the same sender as in the Leroux case... The recipient? The son of the other caretaker, Madame Burot... shocking yes... No, he is alright... Are you coming?"

Verger, the headmaster and Frédéric's teacher solemnly stood around the boy in the playground. Léonie swooped on her son, who cut short any maternal outburst.

"It's a letter for you."

Everybody went into the classroom, now evacuated and quiet. The envelope was lying on the child's desk. On its cover, childlike writing in red crayon and large capital letters stated: 'FOR YOUR MUMMY'. Beaumont opened his attaché case and rubbed his hands.

"Dd'you know what's going to happen? You are going to leave the room and let me do my job. It'll be done quickly..."

Sensible suggestion. The group minus the forensic

expert made their way to the Headmaster's office. There, Fleurus interrogated Frédéric:

"So, how did you discover this letter?"

The child hesitated, anxious not to reveal a behaviour which might be illicit.

"Go ahead! Nobody will scold you."

"It's my friend Lucien. He had given me his doubles from his picture card collection…"

"Uh?"

"The chocolate CO-OP, 'On the trail of American Indians'."

"Great!" the inspector commented with no one knowing if he was expressing a sincere opinion or just coaxing Frédéric.

"I wanted to put them in my satchel. Then I saw…"

"But before that, you hadn't noticed anything? For example yesterday, at home, or this morning in class, when you took out your books…"

"No. It was in my secret compartment…"

"Your secret compartment?"

"Yes. I open it only when I have special things to put in it."

"That makes sense…"

A pause. Salsify turned towards Verger whom Frédéric had not stopped staring at while he was talking.

"Well, I can't really congratulate you. Don't you have any idea how the Chinaman managed to slip this poison into the child's bag?"

"Er… no," muttered the old policeman.

He in turn had been looking at Frédéric; each wanting to make sure that he could trust the other. The Chinaman had of course done it at the Bilboquet. There, what they had omitted to explain the day before, was that not only had they drunk a lemonade but they had also played table football and the boy had left his satchel on a chair behind them. It would have been as easy as pie to sneak a letter into it. But why admit it and give the others a stick to beat them with?

Chapter 54

P AH TURNED UP the next morning. She apologized for her late appearance – she had needed an authorization from the judge – and placed on the bedside table a basket full of provisions: fruit, meat pies, rice pancakes.

"You have to eat. Here, they mustn't give you enough."

She gave him news about the garden. The eggplants were doing well, so were the onions. Soon she would sow some radishes… Her monologue alliterated like a lullaby.

"Is it true that Gabriel… hanged himself?" he interrupted her suddenly.

"Yes," she replied stroking his forehead.

"And Henriette? How is she?"

"She's ill. She wants to see no one."

Was she going to follow her husband into the grave? And what if he, Emile, were to die too? He might let himself waste away, refuse to feed himself. Ferret, with his obscure questions, would be really annoyed! But no, he couldn't abandon Pah, nor Wawa whom the magistrate accused as well.

"D'you know where they've… put Wawa?"

"In prison, I suppose."

Logical, from their point of view. But so foolish from his!

"Do you remember the pictures… we took next to the locomotive?" Although dating back to that ridiculous picnic, these photos had started appearing from deep in his memory, and the desire to have them beside him was rapidly emerging: they belonged to the world of his past, the one he remembered, friendly and tranquil.

"Yes, of course…"

"There are more… Gabriel and me, with Eliane, at the depot… can you bring them to me?"

"Where did you put them?"

It was a while since he had seen them, he was not so sure anymore…

"At work, I think. Go and see Leblanc and ask him to open my office for you."

Chapter 55

"AN ENVELOPE not even sealed!" Beaumont joined them again after less than ten minutes, as annoyed as a mail-order customer receiving poorer quality than he ordered.

"... The first thing I did was to turn over your envelope. Unsealed! Open to the air! Not a good start for a booby-trapped letter. The analyses are negative, from A to Z. I came for nothing."

They went back to the classroom. The forensic expert had taken out the content from its container: a newspaper article cut out from *Le Courrier de Haiphong* dated 8th February 1950. Fleurus and Léonie carefully bent over it, as if expecting a reaction. Not a chemical reaction since the doctor had guaranteed the safety of the envelope in this respect, but rather their reaction to the semantics. A code, a warning...

"Have you read it, Doctor?"

"Of course not!"

His speciality was poisons. The rest, he washed his hands of.

"Let's have a look, then..."

'Press release, from Vladivostok. The Embezzler Casimir de Claret-Llobet is Dead.'

A man, of French nationality, who had checked into a hotel of this Siberian city under the name of Albert Jauguerra, was found stabbed, three days ago. Not a typical victim: found stacked at the bottom of his suitcase were no less than eighteen passports, covering a range of six countries. One of them was in the name of Casimir de Claret-Llobet, and bore multiple chops from the French territory of Guang-Zhou-Wan. Odious crime, vengeance? The violent end of this swindler proves again the saying 'ill got, ill spent.' Unfortunately there remains an unanswered question: will the cash he stole from France ever be found?

A nervous scratching of his head by Fleurus, a grimace from Léonie. She had got it all wrong. Jacques Sergent was not Casimir de Claret-Llobet. "Claret-Llobet? He's been dead for a long time," Pah had shouted at her. And Pioux: "The truth, our document would have clearly revealed it…" She regretted having panicked, wrongly interpreted, refused to listen. But then, if the pseudo railway entrepreneur had been murdered in 1950, who on earth was the man from third floor, flat C?

Chapter 56

J UDGE FERRET, always ploughing the same furrow of time, never interrogated Emile about events *before* the 14th of July. Emile sensed the mistake, without being able to define it clearly. Until, at last, one day:

"The Oliveira brothers, what do you know about them?"

"The Portuguese of Macau?"

"Yes. Well, they're back in Fort-Bayard. I came across them yesterday."

"At The Travellers?"

"No. Madame Vallée being ill, she closed her hotel."

"Ill? Oh yes. My daughter mentioned it… It's not serious, I hope?"

"No. She'll recover."

An assertion which the judge wanted out of the way. He had not come all this way to discuss the health of the friends of an accused person.

"… Now, concentrate please and don't interrupt me. Let us get back to the Oliveiras. You remember that they had supposedly informed Pioux of the presence of Claret-Llobet in Macau. You also recall, on the strength of this information, having decided a kind of punitive expedition against your ex-boss, an expedition which the circumstances fortunately prevented… Yes? Good. I'm delighted that your memory remains faithful to you on this matter and that you don't contradict your friend Wawa, because I am only repeating here a story he told me. I won't mention the perfectly illegal nature of this initiative. The real problem is that the Oliveira brothers yesterday confessed that in fact they had never seen Claret-Llobet in Macau."

"He was under another name... Buffard, or Buffet."

"Nonsense! This too is an invention! They've admitted everything: they wanted to play a trick on Jean Pioux. Knowing what he was like, they were sure it would work. Like the meeting between your Buffet, Dos Santos and Seng: a figment of the imagination. At least partial. There was indeed a meeting... The Farmer General and Seng, I agree. But the third fellow was not Claret-Llobet."

"Who, then?"

"None other than Leblanc, your director. As you can see there is nothing there to be excited about! Be that as it may, the lesson that I learn from all this is that the accusation you made against your former employer is in shreds. In shreds, do you hear?"

"All the better," said Emile.

How could the judge have said that he had accused Claret-Llobet of stealing opium in order to clear himself? Why should he have uttered such an absurdity when it seemed clear that Emile only felt indifference towards the crook?

The judge, more than ever doubting the sanity of his prisoner, adjourned the session. Bouillon then reimmersed himself into the world of his past. In employing him in Customs and Excise, Leblanc had saved him from poverty. What had Ferret said about him? That it was Leblanc and not Claret-Llobet who was in Macau with Dos Santos and Seng? He did not remember any recent visit there by his boss. Pre-war, Leblanc made a point of announcing his slightest movement and of making a report when he returned. Much less punctilious since the defeat, he could indeed have omitted to inform his subordinates. Even so, they would still have noticed his absence. Unless he had travelled on a weekend or during a leave. There again, why would he have sacrificed some of his holidays to go and see Dos Santos and Seng, two individuals whom he totally loathed? In fact, it didn't make sense: during their conversation after the flop of his escapade with Pioux and Gabriel, Leblanc had never mentioned: *It was I who was dining with Dos Santos and Seng at the military Club, and whom the Oliveira brothers mistook for someone else.* No, he merely expressed some doubt regarding the ability of that trio to reproduce a triumph similar to the *Wing On.* Why talk that way, if he knew perfectly well that Seng and Dos Santos had met neither Buffet nor Claret-Llobet, but just himself? There was only one explanation: the Oliveiras had lied all along to Pioux and Ferret. Neither Leblanc nor Dos Santos nor Seng had met up in Macau. Such a meeting had simply never taken place.

Chapter 57

SIXTEEN HUNDRED hours exactly. Léonie turned the key in her lock. Relief: Ernest was not yet back. She left her son at the door, rushed to her note, tore it up and threw it into the rubbish bin.

16:02. She frenetically searched every pocket of her apron. What had she done with the archivist's phone number? Thrown it away? No, the piece of paper was there. Phew!

16:04.

"Hello, Philibert? It's Léonie Burot."

"Ah! Cool."

"Cool, yes. Now, listen to me. In your archives of Fort-Bayard, you're going to take out all the documents concerning everything or almost everything about the following persons... Oh yes...? So you prefer me to write to your superior and inform him that you illegally take out documents...? What am I talking about? About the note you showed me the other day and which you very kindly left the original of, with Inspector Fleurus... Very good! I can see that you understand me perfectly. Do you have a pen and a piece of paper...? Yes, so here goes: Jean Pioux, Emile Bouillon, Gabriel Vallée... that's right, associates of Claret-Llobet and railwaymen, you have a good memory. I continue: Wawa, W A W A, I suppose, Pah, P A H and finally Seng, S E N G, also known as The Lobster, a drug dealer. Let me make things easier for you: don't trouble yourself with the period preceding the railway scandal. What I'm looking for certainly took place after that. You'll bring me all this tomorrow morning, Sunday, at ten, at The

Bilboquet, rue des Bauches... The ministry is closed? Hundreds of pages to examine? And you don't know where rue des Bauches is? Get someone to open up for you, spend the night there if you must, and ask your way to The Bilboquet."

16:09. She briefed her son: "Not a word to your father about what's happened. There's no need to worry him for so little... And you didn't hear a thing of what I've just said to this gentleman. Understood?"

"Er..."

"Next week I'll buy you the fire engine we saw in the shop window before the holidays."

16:10. Ernest entered the lodge.

"They really annoyed me at work. They're all as excited as kids on Christmas morning about this referendum! As if it was going to change anything... And you?"

"Oh, us..."

An ordinary day, all things considered.

Chapter 58

ROARING ENGINES, heavy boots, raised voices… Emile didn't sleep a wink all night. An explanation came from Saunier the next morning:

"That's it, we got clobbered! Guang-Zhou-Wan isn't French anymore. Neither are our concessions in Shanghai, Canton and Backwater-on-Yangtse. The Vichy Government has just returned them to Nankin. The Japs ordered it of course and the nocturnal brouhaha was their soldiers coming to town. Canons, armoured vehicles, troops… The whole caboodle!"

The doctor launched into apocalyptic prophecies: Chiang Kai-Shek was very quickly going to break his diplomatic relationship with Vichy, which had ceded France's possessions in China to China's enemies. And within the next forty-eight hours, Fort-Bayard was going to undergo severe bombing. Bouillon turned pale…

"We've got shelters, don't worry!"

No. It was not Saunier's conjecture of bombing which frightened Bouillon, it was the memory of an earlier conversation which he had just recalled: "It'll soon be a different story… The Japanese will prove to be less easy-going. The culprits, real or not, are going to pay, and dearly!" Who had told him so? Leblanc! Leblanc who had already announced the imminent invasion of the Japanese. But when? These statements shooting at him fell straight away into a deep nothingness, leaving him only with a vague sense of anguish.

Pah's arrival didn't calm him much: she confirmed the presence of the Japanese army all over town.

"I also have news of your pictures. I talked to your boss, as you had asked me to. He found them, he'll bring them himself."

"Really?"

"Yes. You know he's not cross with you concerning…"

She didn't finish her sentence.

Chapter 59

PHILIBERT AT THE Bilboquet, rue des Bauches. Nothing could have been more practical for Léonie on this election Sunday: she was going to vote at her son's school. Alone because Ernest, antagonistic to universal suffrage, had decided, together with a few like-minded colleagues from the printing house, to play a game of petanque in Ranelagh Park.

"Don't expect me for lunch!"

"Why don't you take Frédéric with you?"

The boy clapped his hands. Not that he was passionate about petanque, but many of his friends were to be found in Ranelagh on Sundays. Some great adventures in store! Ernest accepted the suggestion and Léonie was delighted to have elbow room for the whole day.

At the polling station they congratulated her for carrying out her civic duty despite the sorrows of Antoinette's case. Her ballot paper in the box, she immediately went out, walked around the block to make sure that there was no Bricoux on her tail, and entered the Bilboquet. She chose a table away from the bar and the chatting customers. The archivist was not long in coming. His eyes were rheumy, he was pale and his suit was creased. He had stayed up late going through his files.

"What are you drinking?"

He was happy with a café au lait but she would have been willing to buy him something stronger. After a few seconds of an uncomfortable silence, he began:

"I didn't find much. However this letter should interest

you: a story about stealing opium. It gathers together most of your main characters."

Philibert opened the document on the table.

From: Customs and Excise FB/EL
To: General Director of Customs and Excise in Hanoi.
19th July 1943
Dear General Director,
You asked me to write a detailed report on the stealing of a stock of opium from Customs and Excise at Guang-Zhou-Wan which took place 14th inst., attached herewith. I hope by being objective and frank it will meet your expectations. I did not shirk my responsibilities, the first one being to have somewhat put the cat among the pigeons as it was I who recruited Emile Bouillon, former engineer of the short-lived railway of Fort-Bayard against whom all the evidence seems to be directed in this affair.

Should you need any further information, I would be pleased to furnish it.
Yours Sincerely,

This printed letter of introduction bore the signature of a certain Edmond Leblanc, Director of Customs and Excise of the territory of Guang-Zhou-Wan. It already contained one surprise: Bouillon employee of Customs and Excise after his embarrassment at the railway, went from being regarded as a victim... to being a thief! So, what was the report, stapled to this missive, going to reveal?

Chapter 60

A SIREN PIERCED the night and a throbbing sound filled the air. "Planes! They are attacking us!" shouted someone, somewhere. A cannonade. The concerto crescendoed. An explosion, a burning blast, a hail of glass, wood and cement... Emile chose not to look. When he opened his eyes again, his bed was strewn with rubble and a wide hole had replaced the window of his room in which an unpleasant odour of gunpowder was floating. The wail of the siren faded, the ack-ack fire too. Silence, once again... Not for long. The corridor was filled with the hurly-burly of people running in all directions, trolleys, moans, and quite some time later, Saunier.

"What a stroke of luck! Your plaster protected you better than armour. Others haven't been so lucky. Five people dead and twenty wounded in Fort-Bayard. At least for the time being, because they've just started to clear up... I had told you we would be bombed. It happened even more quickly than I thought. Quickly but badly: the Japs didn't suffer any damage. Damn these pilots! It's not even known if they're Yanks or Chinese. Not the sharpest whichever."

Emile saw and heard Saunier as if from very far away, as if he were elsewhere; elsewhere in the past. The deep well that had held the few days stolen from his memory was now releasing them. And these days, so special to him, came back as intact and shiny as jewellery in their casket: his expedition to Eliane on 14th July, the door of the furnace he opened, the crates from Customs and Excise inside, the one he unsealed, the box he removed, his return to Fort-Bayard, Leblanc and Ambroggiani unlocated, The

Travellers where he showed the box to Gabriel, the sudden intervention of the Commander of the Indigenous Guard, their arrest, his fleeing through the worksite, the night when he wandered, his return home early in the morning, Pah, the coffee and the eggs she prepared for him; his whole day alone on the Peak of the Mandarin; his visit to Leblanc, the curious magnificence of his superior's residence, the cognac, the painting, the denunciation of Gabriel's and Wawa's smuggling, the sudden generosity: three thousand piastres; then his hike toward Pointe Nivet, the carriage in which Dos Santos and Seng were riding, the tea house in the night...

They are inside, with their accomplice. He watches them from outside, dying to sleep but he must resist, find out what they are plotting. Now they are coming out. Dos Santos first, his potbelly forward, his side whiskers as shiny as the hair of a fox. Behind him, Seng, his pincer-hands and his protruding eyes. At last the one he is waiting for... Claret-Llobet. He has got his man. He can see him, puffing away on his cigar. He sees him until he comes out of the cloud of smoke enveloping him, until the moonlight reveals his smooth features, until the evidence, which ignites all of a sudden inside his head, makes him realise that... it is Leblanc!

Chapter 61

R EPORT ON THE THEFT OF THE STOCK OF OPIUM FROM FORT-BAYARD WHICH TOOK PLACE ON 14TH JULY 1943

14th July last, having an urgent matter pending, I went to Customs and Excise at around six o'clock in the evening, after the National Day's festivities. Entering the building, I was surprised not to see the guard who normally sat in the lobby. Not paying too much attention to this, I continued to my office. From there, I perceived an unusual noise, a kind of banging. It did not take me long to discover its source: the watchman and his two colleagues whom I found, tied up and muzzled, in a broom cupboard. I freed them and they took me to the storage room where I observed the disaster: all the crates of opium, twenty-two in total, had been stolen. Together we looked to see where the thieves had entered, and discovered that the small side door of the main building had been broken open. Right away this detail disconcerted me: this discreet access leads to a winding corridor which, following a rather strange architectural logic, eventually arrives at the storage room; a long route but a sure one. Had the criminals used an-other entrance, they would have found themselves face to face with the guards. How could they have known about it without being informed from someone on the inside? Then one detail struck me: Emile Bouillon had not shown up at the 14th July festivities which he had never missed in previous years and which he assured me, the day before, he would attend. Fearing that he might be unwell, I had visited his home earlier in the afternoon. He was not there. According to his adopted daughter who let me in, he had gone, that morning, into the jungle of Surprise to tend to the locomotive of the late railway of Fort-Bayard, which had been rotting away for a long time and which he maintained every weekend, moved by some incomprehensible, morbid adoration. This solitary activity sounded like a crude alibi. I talked frankly to Commander Ambroggiani, the chief of the Indigenous Guard, with whom I lodged a complaint. What followed proved me right. In the course of the evening, the commander apprehended Bouillon in possession of a box of opium from the stolen stock, he and those who were his accomplices, thieves with earlier allegations of smuggling: Gabriel Vallée, also a former railwayman, later the proprietor of The Travellers hotel (where in actual fact the arrest took place), and his handyman, a Chinaman known as Wawa. Bouillon's fleeing shortly after his capture was another strong indication of his guilt. He was caught, two days later, with a large sum of money on him: more than three thousand piastres. How had he got hold of these, if not by selling part of the profit of the burglary?

Where do we stand today? Our stocks are still missing. Wawa, the Chinaman, loudly denies guilt. Vallée committed suicide and cannot therefore express himself. As for my ex-employee, he too is not, for the time being, able to talk. During his second arrest he tumbled into a crevasse. Suffering from severe head and spine injuries, he is, temporarily let's hope, amnesiac. The Commander of the Indigenous Guard and Judge Ferret, in charge of the case, for a while believed he was feigning, but Doctor Saunier asserted that he was not. Under these circumstances, Ferret is reluctant to officially charge him.

I fear that the imminent retrocession of Guang-Zhou-Wan to the pro-Japanese government of Nankin may cancel for good all hopes of recovering our opium which the Japanese have constantly coveted since their occupation. The theft made them furious. They or their puppets will take over the inquiry. Should their crude methods allow them to recuperate the goods, I doubt whether they would return them to us…

The following pages dealt with the costs incurred by the damage and questions of insurance. Léonie did not read further. But… She went back to the covering letter written by the man called Edmond Leblanc.

"Come! We'll continue at my place!"

They left the café, the caretaker marching on ahead, the archivist trailing in her wake.

Léonie rushed to her sewing box. She paid no attention to the stupid expression on Philibert's face while he observed her stirring through the small treasures of her private life. There was Joseph's letter, her fiancé in Combreux – he was a really good sort! – and the postcard of the Opera, written by the man from third floor, flat C.

For me too, this melody is like a ray of sunshine into my heart. Jacques Sergent.

"Give me your document again, will you?"

She grabbed it from his hands.

The same well-rounded 'e', the same aggressive 'n' and the same general style… In short, the signature of one and the same man.

Chapter 62

THE CARRIAGE CARRIES the three crooks away from the tea house. Bouillon also leaves. Where to? He does not know. Walk, just keep walking. His mind drifts like flotsam at sea. He feels the Hatamen butt in his pocket. Judge Ferret was right: anybody smokes cigars, including Leblanc, and including that brand. He throws it down, crushes it into the ground with his heel, and resumes walking. There was a winding path on his right. Walk, walk more, walk to the point of being intoxicated. On the horizon, the silhouette of a building. Which one? He recognizes it only when he reaches it: the ice factory. How did he end up here? But on reflection, that's not too bad. He will push on all the way to the chapel on the edge of Surprise and sleep there. Tomorrow, he will go on to Eliane. Never mind if she is guarded, if he gets arrested. All he wants is to see her again.

Suddenly, footsteps. He looks around to see where he could hide but there are nothing but flat paddy fields. A voice calls.

"Hey! You!"

It's Ambroggiani. He flees. He's being chased. A whole troop.

"Stop or I shoot!"

He doesn't obey although he knows he won't be able to go very far, his legs and his lungs are going to give up. Imminent, done: the ground, all of a sudden, is no longer solid. He falls. A shock, a second, a third… His head, his back, his body is breaking apart. Then nothing.

Chapter 63

AT THE ENTRANCE to 14, avenue Velasquez, impeccably polished plaques indicated obscure but undoubtedly lucrative company names: Bauchard and Wellington, Sogetex Ltd, Finalux Ltd, La Zurichoise AG, etc... No EEAC though; the firm preferred discretion.

Léonie rang the bell of the caretaker's lodge.

"Yes? Who is it?"

"I, er... Have I got the right address for the office of EEAC?"

"Just a moment, someone will come..."

Before long the gate opened, behind it stood two men.

"Police, please follow us!"

Léonie found herself in the lift, escorted by the two watchdogs. They stopped on the fourth floor.

"Madame Burot! What a surprise!" welcomed a cheerful Fleurus on the doorstep to her right. "Come in and marvel..."

Pieces of furniture, paintings and sophisticated curios; the opposite of Sergent's interior at rue François Ponsart. Despite the embarrassment of the situation, Léonie, did indeed, marvel.

"The occupant of this five-star pied-à-terre certainly heard us coming. He escaped down the service stairs. But it's only a matter of time before we get him! And this time, we beat you to it. You probably wonder how we did that..."

Salsify was playing the same game he played at Rambouillet.

"The old lady, Madame Burot, her again. You can't always take the word of a policeman at face value. I had complained that after your call she refused to answer my questions. But I'm not the type who gives up easily. I decided to go and see her. The sight of an official ID card often loosens tongues. OK! She told me as much as she told you. So, when you replied to me that Sergent had bought the house in Rambouillet, I knew that you were not telling me the whole truth…"

Léonie wanted to protest.

"… by omission, by not specifying that the property had been purchased not by Sergent but by his company, EEAC, which the old lady had given you the exact details of: this place."

"But…"

"Why this small deception on my part? To see how far you would go! What have you come here for, Madame Burot? To arrest Sergent or to warn him? I don't really know, but it would be better for you to go back home because the case is becoming delicate. It's really not for you anymore. Here, what do you think this is?"

Fleurus had just picked up, from an escritoire, a long sculpted wooden pipe with a silver dragon's head at the end.

"We call it… a pipe?"

"A pipe, yes. But not an ordinary pipe. An opium pipe!"

"Jesus, Mary! D'you know… I think I know the real identity of Jacques Sergent."

"If it's nonsense…"

"No. In fact his name is Edmond Leblanc. He was the Director of Customs and Excise in Fort-Bayard, where, as it happens, what you're holding, was made."

"Good God! Come to CID tomorrow morning at eight o'clock!"

"How about my job?"

"Resign!"

Chapter 64

"HOW ARE YOU feeling?"

His pulse was being taken by Saunier. But he was surprised to be on a stretcher on the floor, around which strolled half a dozen pairs of legs, the owners of which were bending down to be at his level: Amyot, Father Cellard, etc.

"Were are we?"

"In prison. You fainted during your transfer."

He saw the walls stained with moisture, the heavy steel door with its wire screened small window. Leblanc's prediction was coming true. The Japanese were taking over the administration of justice… But what were the others doing in the cell?

"All the French have been arrested."

"But why?"

"Lefébure…"

Taking advantage of the chaos caused by the air raid, the Commander of the 19th and his men had gone over to China, taking with them their guns and, on the way, killing three soldiers of the Rising Sun. In order to prevent further incidents, the Japanese had imprisoned all the French.

"Even Abusive Curt! But he is entitled special treatment. He's been put up in a private cell…"

"How about Leblanc?"

A mystery. He too had gone. Opinions differed. His political views were unknown but couldn't he have joined Lefébure? Unless he perished…

"A bomb exploded not far from his villa. Three or four burnt bodies were found and lots of body parts, impossible to identify them. God knows if he was among them?" added Saunier.

"He didn't return my pictures," grumbled Emile.

Nothing more. Who would have believed him had he asserted that Leblanc was the instigator of the theft of the opium of Customs and Excise, and that his accomplices were Seng and Dos Santos?

Chapter 65

THE TYPEWRITER OF good old Bergeron was clicking away like a vibraphone in a stochastic music concert. Léonie sat down in the one-armed chair. Fleurus handed over a rectangle of creased paper to her.

"*Le Soir de Hanoi...* taken from Pioux's pile of documents."

"An article to read, like at school?"

"Yes, it relates Claret-Llobet's death in Siberia. Pioux asserts that it is what he wanted to show you the other day, and not to 'gun you down'. I remain cautious, but the fact is that this thief was sent to his maker in 1950. Sergent is someone else. Yesterday, you suggested a name..."

"Edmond Leblanc. Former Director of Customs and Excise of Fort-Bayard."

"May we know where you got it from, this one?"

"From the archives, me too..."

With an enigmatic smile, the caretaker dissuaded Fleurus from trying to go deeper into the subject.

"I found a different document to yours: a note, bearing the signature of that gentleman. As it happens, I'm not unfamiliar with the signature of Jacques Sergent," she said without mentioning the postcard. "Both seemed very similar to me."

"And this note, what did it say?"

"It talked about a theft of opium."

Léonie summed up the details, before concluding:

"In actual fact, I believe it was Leblanc who was guilty of that crime."

Fleurus fixed her with a stare like that of an Indian cobra.

"During the interrogation, the bunch from Rambouillet gave me the same story. I telephoned the Minister of Overseas France. A Mr. Edmond Leblanc did once occupy the post of Director of Customs and Excise in Fort-Bayard before disappearing in strange circumstances in August 1943. He was never found again. He's officially in the category of missing persons. A nonentity."

"They told you his date of birth?"

"Yes… 9th June 1901."

"That's Jacques Sergent's! I know it," Léonie exulted whilst refraining, as with the postcard, from giving too much detail.

"If what you say is true, everything makes sense. But come, let's have a coffee. Somewhere where we won't be disturbed."

Bergeron turned around, annoyed. It was *they* who were disturbing *him* with their Abbott and Costello patter.

Corridors, stairs… all the way to a tiny room divided by a Formica counter behind which a lightly moustachioed barmaid with gibbon-like arms was protectively sweeping cups, saucers and spoons to her breast, as if the four or five colleagues of Fleurus's who were drinking in front of her while discussing wage rates, were likely, at any moment, to turn into incorrigible looters.

"This is Madame Burot, my main witness in the Leroux case. Berthier, Lucas, Astier, Nicolleau…" Salsify seemed not a little proud to introduce Léonie: main witnesses like her one did not come across every day. Once they got their coffee, they settled close to a radiator which they used as a table.

"Where were we?"

"Leblanc's date of birth. The same as Jacques Sergent's."

"Ah! yes, that's funny. And so is EEAC. Again I

approached Interpol, and my colleagues in Luxembourg since that company is registered there…"

The policeman put his cup down and flipped through his notebook.

"Here it is. *Company created on 19th June 1946. Company purpose: import-export…* Banal, but what follows is less so: property renovation and management."

"Like in Rambouillet!?"

"Not so fast! I'll come back to it. First, the shareholders. There are three of them. Jacques Sergent…"

That goes without saying.

"Seng… the poisons expert…"

"God!"

"And a Portuguese, a certain Dos Santos, former Head of the Tax Farm in Macau, an operation rather similar to Customs and Excise in Fort-Bayard, from what I gathered. Officially retired, he still lives over there…"

Head of the Tax Farm, Léonie imagined a kind of tyrannical landowner, reigning over enslaved masses.

"We've got the setting and the cast. The first act was in Austria, six years ago…"

"Really?"

"A pile-up on a road not far from Vienna, on a foggy day… In one of the cars, emergency aid stumbles on a small arsenal of opium pipes and opium lamps. The driver, a Burmese national, lives in a detached house at the edge of a forest. The police search it. There, more pipes, more lamps, bunks and all the related paraphernalia. Enough to set up an authentic opium den. Only the drug was missing. As a result of which the person was not that much concerned. Neither was his sponsor who, I bet you'll never guess, was none other than…"

"EEAC!"

"Which had bought these goods two months previously, and sold them on one week after the incident…"

"Rambouillet!" shouted Léonie again. "They wanted to do the same thing in Rambouillet!"

"I wouldn't be too surprised. Also elsewhere in Europe. It's not only in the Orient that wealthy amateurs take to this kind of vice. I checked with Air France. Sergent is one of their best customers. Berlin, Amsterdam, London, Athens… these are the places where he goes when he is absent from Paris. Three or four day trips, you had noticed yourself. He probably supervises the houses, and Seng and Dos Santos are engaged in providing him with opium, because if it's an opium den we are indeed dealing with, the initial stock stolen in Fort-Bayard must have run out some time ago. The problem with crooks is that they are short-tempered and tight-fisted. Their associations quickly experience frictions. Sergent and his accomplices must have quarrelled, the latter wanting to get rid of the former. With the booby trapped letter…"

"Yes but… what about the people in Rambouillet in all this?"

"Go-betweens, executioners… They had good reason for wanting to take their revenge on Leblanc."

"Not Pioux. He had nothing to do with the theft of the opium. And what would Seng and Dos Santos have needed him and his employees for?"

Fleurus stiffened.

"Pioux and his associates are giving me that line too," he softened after a moment. "They deny any relationship with Seng and Dos Santos and claim they bumped into Leblanc in a street in Rambouillet, last June, at the time he purchased his house. So let's consider this some more…"

Léonie approved. She too had always thought that theirs

had been a chance encounter.

"So they, worried, curious, whatever you like… they tail him. It's the episode when Wawa was at your place, discovering that their man's name from now on is Jacques Sergent. But, after that, things drift apart. The photos in the letter supposedly belonged to Bouillon. Leblanc allegedly stole them from him at the end of the war, or at least forgot to return them to him. This is unlikely. If Sergent had them in his possession, how could anyone have posted them to him from Hong Kong and, what's more, covered with poison? As a matter of fact, after I pointed this out to them, they didn't say anything more."

Cannot words hide the truth better than silence, when the audience is not able to hear?

"Jesus-Mary!" cried out Léonie almost spilling her coffee. "Can we go and see Doctor Beaumont?"

Chapter 66

THEIR SUDDEN APPEARANCE disconcerted the forensic doctor.

"Are you bringing me another letter?"

"No."

"What can I do for you, then?"

"It's about the poison that killed Antoinette Leroux," started Léonie. "I remember you considered that the steam increased the strength of the toxicity…"

"Exactly. It melted the gelatin which solidified the deadly mixture of Etorphine and Lewisite, dispersed it and occasioned the direct contamination of her airways."

"But… at what temperature does gelatin melt?"

"Not so high. Think of jelly beans, they melt in the mouth at 37 degrees, the temperature of the human body. And even at a lower degree nowadays, for the manufacturers are making advances all the time: hardly more than 30 degrees. In fact there is one detail I didn't explain, in my report, but remember the envelope in your bunch of mail. Its padding served to insulate it; without doubt to prevent the gelatin from melting during the journey, especially at the beginning, in Hong Kong, in the tropics…"

"So, had my friend open the letter, not in her lodge with steam but in an overheated greenhouse where a fan and an atomizer were constantly switched on…"

"The effect would have been less brutal but Madame Leroux would then have had more time left to handle the photos. Because, as it happens, Lewisite acts through the skin…"

"She still would have died?"

"Probably."

"And what if there had been four people present in the room?"

"The doses released could have killed the weakest ones and made marshmallow of the strongest."

"This is how I see it," said Léonie after thanking the forensic doctor. "In Rambouillet, Pioux's gang spots Leblanc. And for his part Leblanc realises that his old compatriots from Fort-Bayard have taken up residence there. Aware of his past and his true identity, they constitute a danger the more serious for him since he has bought a house just a few steps away from theirs to carry out his nefarious activities. Not allowing himself to take any risk, he decides to do away with them. We must believe Bouillon: his former boss is in possession of his photographs. The enigma then is easily solved. Leblanc entrusts them to his associate Seng from Hong Kong who coats them with poison and sends them back to him. But their final destination is to be Rambouillet. A new envelope with a French stamp will not arouse any suspicion in the horticulturists. They will open this apparently harmless letter. Bouillon will recognize his pictures. Wawa and Pah will see themselves next to other figures from the past: Gabriel Vallée, his wife Henriette, the locomotive Eliane. Pioux too will show some interest. The pictures will go round. 32 degrees Celsius in the room, where the atomizer and the fan are humidifying and circulating the air. The gelatin melts, the poison spreads and runs down onto the hands of the victims…"

Like the tears running down the caretaker's cheeks, induced by her dramatic reconstruction of the events.

"Well done Madame Burot! A beautiful explanation!"

Fleurus congratulated her. "The booby-trapped letter passing through Sergent's address in Paris, impossible to trace Seng and Dos Santos in Hong Kong. With the photos, one, on the contrary, searches in the direction of the railway and Fort-Bayard. One is led back to Claret-Llobet. He is dead. One definitely gets stuck. Without the unfortunate interception of the envelope by the too curious Madame Leroux, the whole saga would never have come to light."

The time had come. Léonie breathed in deeply.

"I have to confess one thing… I lied to you. The too curious caretaker… it was me."

Fleurus did not comment. Coming out of Beaumont's office, he sent out an international warrant for the arrest of Edmond Leblanc, alias Jacques Sergent, Manuel Dos Santos and Seng Loon-Fat.

Epilogue

PEACE ARRIVED. The Japanese left the Colony. Chiang Kai-Shek, rejecting the Vichy decision to cede it back to Nankin, returned it to the French government, which, in its turn, gave it back to him. Freed from the Japanese prisons like most of his countrymen, Emile was reunited with Pah. She told him of the death of Henriette. This news was not exactly a morale booster. Deeply affected, he sank into depression. Wawa too came out of prison. Having nothing to do, he entered the Nationalist Army. The nigh indestructible *Hué* took the colonists back to Indochina. Bouillon and his daughter met Ferret on the ship. Pah sounded out the judge:

"Will my father stand trial, over there?"

"Not sure. Considering his condition and the general chaos… The Nankin flunkeys confiscated all my files. Starting the inquiry all over again wouldn't make much sense. We wouldn't have enough witnesses, evidence…"

Ferret was right. They were never troubled. Lodging in barracks in Hanoi, they one day had the surprise of seeing Jean Pioux arrive. His business of horticulture was taking off well again. Did they want to work with him? His nurseries were situated at the edge of the Lake of the West. Pah learned the techniques of acclimatisation and reproduction of plants, in which she became an expert of some renown. Her father, at her side, was breathing in the intoxicating perfume of the flowers all day long.

October 1949. The Nationalists were defeated, Wawa fled to Tonkin. His friends welcomed him. Pioux employed him as an assistant.

8th February 1950. The horticulturist religiously cut out all the Indochinese newspapers' articles relating the death of Claret-Llobet in Siberia.

November 1950. Pioux, after the French defeat in Cao Bang, gathered his team.

"Things are starting to go wrong. How about if we go back to France?"

He had just inherited a house in Rambouillet. They settled there.

During a lunch of reconciliation in Rambouillet, Wawa initiated Frédéric in the use of chopsticks and Pioux Ernest, in the finer points of snake alcohol. Léonie gave the dibber back to Pah who was as delighted as if she had won the jackpot in the lottery.

"My talisman. I always carry it around with me."

Nice people. Léonie remembered the world she had imagined they lived in: criminals thirsty for revenge. But no, they more or less shared the same preoccupations, the same joys and pains. Didn't humanity everywhere engender a rather depressing banality? Sergent did not escape from this depression either: an impenetrable gentleman when it suited him, but what, if not the simple fear of being thrown into jail, had driven him to want to get rid of his enemies?

As the whole building and beyond was praising Léonie for her role in the inquiry, Madame Belval was forced to withdraw her petition. Not in the least embarrassed, the nephew contacted her again for an interview. She sent him packing. But was it by remaining at rue François Ponsart that she would best cultivate the wisdom for which she was now getting the credit? She envisaged a new job. With the police, as Salsify had jokingly suggested? Not really for her. Flowers on the other hand… She paid another visit to Pah in Rambouillet and Blanche at the greenhouses in Auteuil, and signed up for a gardening course at the *École Municipale d'Horticulture* in Paris.

Fleurus, while conducting a search of the premises of EEAC, avenue Vélasquez, came across *The Conquest of Guang-Zhou-Wan*, published by Dubreuil, 1901. A fascinating small book, a firsthand account, since it had been written by the Commander of the *Surprise* himself, a certain Captain Jacques Sergent.

Ah! Final details, the omission of which would be a mistake:

In France, the 'Yes' votes for the Fifth Republic won with an overwhelming majority of 85%.

In China, Fort-Bayard was renamed Zhanjiang. In 1958, while clearing up the jungle of Surprise, the zealous followers of the Great Leap Forward unearthed Eliane whose rusty steel was then used as raw material by a factory making nuts and bolts. A French oil company briefly came back to the region in the 1980s: offshore deposits near the islands of Donghai and Naozhou looked promising. The drilling did not produce very much. It must be written somewhere that Guang-Zhou-Wan would never be a successful venture for France.

By the same author
(Under the pen name Fan Tong)

Out of Time in Wan Chai, Blue Lettuce Publishing, 2012